"FROM THE BOTTOM OF MY BLACK HEART" . . .

"I, Harlan James, publicly announce that I will not submit to trial in the racist-pig court of the racist-pig Judge Wendell Graham on the phony charge of sedition framed by a racist-pig district attorney . . .

"I have gone underground to protect myself . . .

"The tape accompanying this letter contains a message to my black brothers and sisters. I DEMAND you play it over the air . . ."

THE TAPE IS PLAYED—A DRASTIC MURDER ENSUES—AND TROUBLESHOOTER MIKE McCALL IS PLUNGED INTO A CASE THREATENING THE LIFE OF A CITY!

ELLERY QUEEN
THE BLACK HEARTS MURDER

MAGNUM BOOKS · NEW YORK

A LANCER BOOK

THE BLACK HEARTS MURDER

LANCER BOOKS INC. • 18 EAST 41ST STREET
NEW YORK, N.Y. 10017

ONE

During the flight downstate from the capital, McCall gave the pamphlet shoved in his hand by Governor Holland a thorough going-over. It had been put out by the Banbury Chamber of Commerce, and as far as McCall could see it was the usual C. of C. pap, studded with statistics like raisins in gruel. According to the Chamber, Banbury was the third most important industrial city in the state, boasting a variety of industries ranging from auto parts and brass mills to roadside electronics firms. Its population according to the 1960 census was 240,972, the Chamber noted, but the projection for 1970 was over 297,000 because of the influx of three more major heavy-industry plants. There was a considerable diversity of ethnic groups among the citizenry, about which the boost-Banbury pamphleteer seemed a little defensive, as if he were not quite sure whether this was a good thing or a bad thing. Relations "between the races," he pointed out in something like haste, were "excellent." The last "trouble," as he put it (McCall had always heard it referred to as a race riot) had occurred in the '20s.

The Assistant to the Governor for Special Affairs was more interested in the black-white breakdown. He found the ratio given in 8-point type in a footnote: "It is estimated that the present proportion of Negro to white citizens in the city of Banbury is in the neighborhood of 24%." That meant over 70,000 blacks.

Sizable.

The numbers made McCall thoughtful. He was flying to Banbury at Governor Holland's behest with the specified mission ("which some of my reports, Mike," the governor had said, "say ought to be called *Mission: Impossible*") of trying to avert a racial explosion. It was predicted that if it came (two of the governor's advisers used the word "when"), its violence would rock the whole state and throw out rivers of political lava.

McCall tossed the Chamber of Commerce brochure aside and leaned back to think the situation through. Few problems, he felt, were impervious to solution. But before courses of action could be plotted, the facts had to be grasped. Where human beings were concerned, he had found, this was rarely a simple task.

There were always wheels within wheels. The coming mayoralty election in Banbury was not the customary local party hassle. Governor Holland's choice for the top job in the city, Jerome Duncan, was sure to lose, and lose heavily, if McCall's mission to bring peace to the troubled city failed. This could result in the defeat of the governor and his party in the next statewide election. (Which in turn, McCall thought with a wry smile, would put me out of a job, too.)

He had never seen Sam Holland so grave as during his briefing before take-off.

"It's not merely my political future and the success of the party I'm concerned about, Mike," the governor had said. "Win or lose two years from now, I wouldn't be able to sleep nights thinking I could somehow have stopped a blood bath and didn't. I don't want such a thing either on my conscience or in my record. I'm vain enough to want to go down as one of the better governors of this state."

"You've already insured that," McCall had said.

"You think so?" Governor Holland had answered grimly. "Let the whites and blacks leave bloody white and black bodies strewn all over the streets of Banbury and see how fast the historians would call me a bum. But what am I talking about? The hell with me. I don't want

6

people killed there, Mike. It's that simple. Though how are you going to stop a head-on collision if Harlan James is convicted . . . You'd have to pull a miracle."

McCall had said, "Haven't you heard, Governor? Miracle is my middle name," speaking with a cheeriness he was very far from feeling.

Harlan James was the fiery leader of the black militant organization in Banbury who called themselves the Black Hearts. He was under indictment, charged with violating the state sedition law. The charge alleged that at the Black Hearts "school for revolutionaries" James had taught his novices how to make bombs and explosive cocktails out of everyday materials; that, furthermore, he had preached to his students the necessity of blowing up those "honky" business establishments, both in and out of the Banbury ghetto, which were guilty of discriminatory hiring practices.

Until his briefing McCall had assumed that the Banbury authorities had substantial grounds for bringing the black leader to trial. But his information, Governor Holland told McCall, was that the indictment of James was largely a political ploy by the opposition party.

"Mayor Potter can't make any public statements about the James case prior to the trial, of course," the governor had said. "But privately he's informed me that he believes James is being framed. He says the district attorney, that weasel Volper, is deliberately trying to promote race trouble in Banbury so that his fair-haired boy, Horton, will be swept into office by the white backlash under his ringing law-and-order slogan. This is a bad time for old Potter to be retiring from politics. Even at his age he could beat Horton. But Jerome Duncan, for all his ability and charm, is a black man, and if there's racial violence before the election, the blue-collar whites are absolutely certain to vote against him."

Until the last election, for an entire generation Heywood Potter's machine had consistently delivered the Banbury vote to the governor's party. But Mayor Potter had grown old, and four years earlier his iron political grip on the city had weakened. Gerald Horton, who owned local radio station BOKO, had been elected city councilman-at-large, and an obscure lawyer named Volper had sneaked out of the political woodwork and smear-talked his way to a surprising victory over the incumbent district attorney. His opponent was a quiet and conscientious prosecutor who had done his job quietly and conscientiously for sixteen years and he promptly, after his defeat, suffered a coronary occlusion and went to his quiet reward. Since Horton's and Volper's victories the opposition had steadily gathered momentum, until now it was ready to make a serious run against the party in power in the race for all city and county offices.

Mayor Potter was eighty-four; his announcement that he would not run again had created a vacuum in his party's primary contest for the mayoral candidacy. Into the vacuum stepped Governor Holland and, with some prodding from the governor's mansion, Heywood Potter. They endorsed Jerome Duncan. (The backroom talk in the capital was that old Heywood had growled, "Hell, Sam, it's not his color—you know me better than that—it's that he can't win," and the governor had said, "I think he can, given the right support, and you and I, Heywood, are the right support.") The party strategists grumbled, but Mayor Potter talked of how much Jerome Duncan resembled Carl B. Stokes in looks and charisma (an argument which impressed everyone but himself), and Duncan easily won the nomination in the primary.

On cold analysis his chance of winning the city election was another matter entirely. Duncan was a widely respected lawyer and he was state president of the

NAACP, but he had little political experience. He could be expected to get a virtually solid black vote, but it was calculated that he needed more than 25% of the city's white vote to be elected, and he was not well known in the lower-class white community. To compound the candidate's difficulties, Harlan James of the Black Hearts had endorsed Duncan's candidacy before his indictment on the sedition charge, gaining Duncan no new support and, as the party pundits saw it, almost certainly losing him substantial blue-collar support among the white voters.

Duncan's opponent was Councilman-at-Large Gerald Horton, who was promising "law'norder" if he were elected, "your wives and sweethearts safe in our streets again," and making capital of his four years in city government as contrasted with Duncan's "cluttering up our court calendars with frivolous suits in support of black power!"

Horton's campaign of fear and Volper's prosecution threat against Harlan James, darling of the black militants, had leaped the gap like a spark, inflaming whites and blacks alike and setting the races at each other's throats. Racial clashes were no longer confined to occasional outbreaks of violence between groups of high school teenagers. Adults were now involved. The wildest rumors ran through Banbury's streets. Mayor Potter had to resort to frequent visits to the municipal radio station to make personal pleas for public calm. There were demonstrations by black workers, demonstrations by white workers, seething picket lines, eruptions of brick-throwing at police and firemen, in short a continuous ferment in the city. It was generally agreed that if it were not for Jerome Duncan, the National Guard would already be occupying the city. The black candidate was everywhere at once, soothing whites, quietly telling

9

blacks to "cool it," that violence was what the racists wanted . . . managing somehow to keep the lid on the rattling pot.

"But it's only a question of time, Mike," Governor Holland's parting words had been to McCall, "when the lid's going to blow off, and then all hell breaks loose. For God's sake find some way to stop it, or at least control it, until after Election Day. I think then it will simmer down."

McCall's plane landed at the municipal airport at 8:10 A.M. At 8:30 he was headed for the county courthouse in a rented Ford. There was no time to pay a courtesy call on the mayor; the trial of Harlan James was scheduled to begin at nine o'clock, and it was a twenty-minute drive from the airport to downtown Banbury.

He had the car radio adjusted to 1410, the frequency of Gerald Horton's station; he wanted to hear what Horton's official line was on the trial of the black leader. It turned out that BOKO broadcast local news on the hour, which he had missed, and devoted the half-past-the-hour news summaries to national and international news, which told him nothing about the Harlan James affair. By the time he had realized this and tried other stations, McCall missed their local newscasts, too.

He swore and turned off the radio.

The county courthouse faced a plaza, and the plaza was jammed with people, almost all black men. One out of every four or five of these black men wore a glittering black vinyl jacket with a circular white insignia on the back. Centered in the white circle was a black heart, and piercing the black heart was a dagger—white.

It was the first time McCall had seen the Black Hearts' emblem, although he had read what meager literature existed on its history. According to an FBI report he had

10

read—labeled "possibly apocryphal"—both the name of the black militant organization and its symbol had been inspired by a U.S. Senate speech delivered by a southern segregationist after the original Supreme Court decision desegregating public schools. The senator was supposed to have said (the quotation had never been found in the *Congressional Record*): "The gleaming white dagger of southern chivalry should be plunged into the black hearts of those responsible for this dastardly murder of human rights."

The story ran that Harlan James, then a boy of twelve, had overheard a discussion of the senator's speech between his parents during which his father commented bitterly, "By human rights he means the rights of Lord-a-mighty whites. We sho'ly ain't human in his eyes."

His father's remark reputedly sank into the young black's memory, to surface in 1968 when the then newly formed black militant group under his leadership was groping for a name. The turnabout use of the senator's metaphor in the black cause delighted Banbury's black community, regardless of individual views, and dismayed whites of all persuasions. James shrewdly played variations on his theme in his speeches. He repeatedly used the terms "black-hearted" as synonymous with "evil" and "white" with "virtuous" in his broad satiric attacks on white racist attitudes and actions. But then, in his perorations, he never failed to make clear what he really meant: "From the depths of my black heart I thank the Lord God that no one has ever said to me, 'That's white of you, Harlan,' and got away with it—'cause white, not black, is the true color of evil!"

Some of the wearers of the Black Hearts jackets were carrying signs. Their messages ranged from a simple FREE HARLAN through a belligerent HONKY FRAME-UP! to one savage D.A. VOLPER AND JUDGE GRAHAM ARE RACIST PIGS.

11

McCall parked his rented car in a side street off the plaza, well away from the courthouse crowd. There were police lines set up behind wooden barricades on the courthouse steps, and he had more trouble getting through these than through the pack of people in the plaza. He managed to, finally, by the open sesame which he disliked using: the unique gold shield identifying him as the governor's special assistant.

Inside the courthouse there was pandemonium. In spite of police efforts, an overflow throng for whom there was no room in the courtroom crammed the corridors and stairway to the upper floor. Somehow McCall made his way against the stream, like a salmon, and eventually found himself in the front rank of the crowd before the courtroom marked 2A. The double door was shut and two brawny marshals had their backs to it.

A young man in a Black Hearts jacket and a dowdy middle-aged white woman were in the vanguard of those at the doors, apparently the first to be denied entrance. They were alternately arguing with the marshals and glaring at each other.

McCall used his open sesame again. The gold governor's seal and the legend beneath made the nearer marshal look at McCall sharply.

"Here's a real live one, Bill," he said to his fellow marshal. "Let this gentleman through." One of the doors opened no more than twelve inches. As McCall wriggled through the narrow opening he heard someone behind him say, "Can you tie that? How come you let that honky in and we have to cool it out here?" and the marshal's rejoinder, "That honky happens to be Mr. McCall, the governor's representative. Stand back!"

It was now several minutes past nine o'clock, but the judge's bench was still unoccupied. The large courtroom sounded full of bees. Every seat in the spectator's section was filled. A single line of standees ranged against the

12

rear wall; the middle and side aisles had been kept clear. The spectators seemed evenly divided between whites and blacks; by contrast with the crowd outdoors, about one black in three wore a Black Hearts jacket. The aisles were patrolled by nervous-looking policemen, almost half of whom were black.

McCall spotted an empty chair in the press section down front, the only unoccupied one in the courtroom. He promptly made his way down the center aisle. A bailiff stopped him at the gate, and McCall had to flash his shield again. It won him the seat.

Seven men and one woman sat in the press section, the woman sitting next to the empty chair McCall had taken. He smiled at her, and she returned the smile with frank curiosity. She was slim, almost gaunt, the tweedy type, a quite attractive brunette somewhere around thirty. She had the lustrous dark eyes and high Indian cheekbones that he always found himself drawn to in a woman, although it had been said that the varieties of feminine attractions to which McCall was drawn rivaled Heinz's products.

"Hi," she said in a friendly voice. "I'm Maggie Kirkpatrick of the Banbury *Post-Telegram*. Who are you?"

"Mike McCall."

"Out-of-town paper or one of the wire services? I don't think I've seen you before."

He shook his head. "I'm not a reporter."

"Mike McCall." The black eyes shimmered. "You don't mean it! Is the Mike short for some name other than Michael?"

"Micah."

"That's it! I can never remember it. Don't tell me you're really the notorious Assistant for Special Affairs to the Governor?"

McCall grinned. "Explain the 'notorious.'"

13

"I wasn't referring to your exploits as Sam Holland's troubleshooter," Maggie Kirkpatrick said, grinning back. "I was referring to your reputation for *l'amour*."

"You're a rotten newspaperwoman if you believe every rumor you hear."

"This one seems awfully persistent. The story goes that every belle in the capital has drawn a bead on you, and every mama of same gets down on her quaking knees nightly and prays that her daughter will get you to the altar before you con her into bed."

"If so, I haven't been caught yet."

"You're supposed to be as slithery as an eel."

"Try me," McCall said. "You'll find I'm easy to catch."

"For what purpose?" Maggie Kirkpatrick retorted.

"Aha," McCall said mysteriously, and his smile closed the door on the subject. He looked around him and began studying the courtroom personnel.

While he made his inspection, the newspaperwoman inspected him with quickening interest and admiration, as most women did. McCall did not impress people, men or women, as a big man, which was more a matter of porportion than size, as in most natural athletes. He was muscled grace even in repose. He had played halfback at Northwestern, and he had never permitted himself afterward to backslide physically. He had a solid, rugged face, the kind other men could not understand women considering handsome, and his dark hair had just the right premature sprinkling of salt.

Maggie Kirkpatrick sighed and looked away. Mama, she thought, if you were still with us you'd be down on your knees right now.

McCall was paying particular attention to the contending tables. At the prosecution table sat two white men. One was plump and pink, with big wet eyes and a sandy gray crewcut. The other was obviously his assistant, a young man, nervous. The defense table was occu-

14

pied by a lone man, black, wearing a conservative blue business suit and a dark gray silk tie; he kept shuffling through the papers before him and casting worried glances over at the courtroom clock.

Maggie Kirkpatrick said, "The two gents with the white skin are District Attorney Volper—he's the pink slug with the fat eyes—and one of his assistant D.A.s. The Negro—excuse me, black—man at the defense table is Harlan James's lawyer, Prentiss Wade."

"Where's his client?" McCall asked.

Maggie shrugged. "Out on ten-thousand-dollar bond, and I think Wade is beginning to sweat. He has an assistant, too, and a few minutes ago he sent him off on an errand. Probably to get on the phone and find out why James isn't here yet. This may be starting off with a bang."

Before McCall could comment, the bailiff rapped, "All rise!" and the judge flapped onto the dais from chambers.

TWO

Judge Graham was a frail-looking man with a stubborn jaw and unruly white hair that made McCall think of the late Senator Dirksen. Court had barely been declared in session—people were still reseating themselves —when a studious-looking young black man hurried into the courtroom, flung himself into a chair at the defense table, and whispered urgently to Prentiss Wade. The black lawyer looked appalled.

The judge was frowning, having noticed that the defendant was not at the defense table. He said to Wade, "Counselor, where is your client?"

The black attorney jumped to his feet. "Your Honor, the arrangement was for Mr. James to meet me here at a quarter of nine this morning. He didn't appear. My associate, Mr. Barker here, has just talked on the phone to the two persons closest to my client. Mr. James's sister, with whom he lives, reports that he did not come home last night and that she has not heard from him. The other person Mr. Barker talked to was LeRoy Rawlings, vice president of the Black Hearts and my client's most loyal friend. Mr. Rawlings has not heard from Mr. James either, and has no idea where he is. I know my client had every intention of being here, Your Honor, so he can only have been delayed by some unforeseen circumstance. I beg the court's indulgence for a few more minutes."

Judge Graham glanced at the clock. "It is now nearly a quarter past nine, Mr. Wade. I will grant you fifteen minutes for more calls to attempt to learn what has happened to the defendant." He used his gavel. "Court is recessed until nine-thirty A.M."

"All rise!" the bailiff bellowed.

The judge headed for his chambers. A uniformed man intercepted him and whispered briefly in his ear. He turned immediately to the attorneys standing behind their tables. "I have a message to contact the chief of police concerning the defendant. I suggest that neither the prosecutor nor defense counsel leaves the courtroom until I determine what this is all about."

Ten minutes later Judge Graham reappeared. He seemed angry and puzzled. "Mr. Wade, I have just talked by telephone with Chief of Police Condon. Chief Condon reports to me that some thirty minutes ago he received a call from radio station BOKO. I will not burden you with the details of BOKO's summary of the situation, because I wish to hear them myself—BOKO intends to give a complete airing of the matter during a special news broadcast at 9:50 A.M. I shall listen to the broadcast on the radio in my chambers, and you gentlemen of both the prosecution and the defense are invited to listen with me. Suffice it to say for the present that I am assured by Chief Condon that the defendant will not appear in this courtroom today, and that his absence is deliberate, an act of naked defiance of this court."

The black lawyer said quickly, "I'm sorry, Your Honor. The court has my assurance that I had no idea or warning that my client planned to skip bail. In fact, I find it very difficult to believe, with due apologies to the court and the chief of police."

"I understand your feelings perfectly, counselor, and you have my sympathy for having been placed in this position. However, from the report I just got, there seems no possible doubt about the fact." In a very sharp voice Judge Graham then said, "Defendant's bail is hereby ordered forfeit. Further, I am issuing a bench warrant for his arrest. Court adjourned! Gentlemen?"

"What do you think, Mr. McCall?" Maggie Kirkpatrick asked in the confusion and babble of the emptying courtroom.

"Make it Mike and I'll tell you, Miss Kirkpatrick."

"If you'll make it Maggie."

"Maggie."

"Mike. Now answer my question."

"What's to think?" McCall smiled. He was far from smiling inside. "I'm the world's lousiest guesser." He glanced at his wristwatch. "That broadcast comes on in eleven minutes."

"Do you have a radio in your car?"

"Yes."

"Then we have plenty of time—"

"Not so. I'm not parked in the courthouse lot. I took one look at that mob in the plaza and left the car on a side street."

Maggie jammed her notebook into her super-giant-sized handbag and seized his arm. "Then let's shake it. What are you doing in Banbury anyway, Mike?" she demanded as they hurried toward the door. "What's Sam Holland's angle on Harlan James?"

"Obvious," McCall said. "The governor wants to stop trouble in Banbury."

"What's this about the governor?" It was one of the other newspaper people, a man with outstanding ears.

"Private conversation, George," Miss Kirkpatrick said with a sweet smile, steering McCall elsewhere. "Here, I know another way out."

She led him down a rear stairway.

"Thanks," McCall said. "I'd rather not conduct a press conference just yet."

"Don't thank me, Mike. My motive is strictly selfish. I want an exclusive."

"Sure you do. But why should I give it to you?"

18

"Because the *Post-Telegram* and I are on the governor's side, and the other newspapers in Banbury aren't. The *Press-Times* would strangle its collective children to sell another paper, so they're all for trouble, the more sensational the better; the *News-Mirror* is lock, stock and barrel in Gerry Horton's camp. And the outside papers don't count. That adds up to let's-you-and-me-play-ball on my scorecard. How about you?"

"You plead a persuasive case," McCall said. "Okay, I'll check your information out, and if you're leveling you've got a deal."

"I'm leveling," Maggie Kirkpatrick said.

He made a snap decision; her ice-gray eyes had remoteness, but not dishonesty. "Shake," he said.

She shook his hand like a man. "I'm taking this to mean you'll keep no secrets from me."

"Whoa, Maggie," McCall smiled. "I didn't agree to any such thing. My book says 'exclusive' means that when I decide to tell the media anything I'll let you in on it first."

Maggie shrugged. "Can't blame a girl for trying. Do you remember my name?"

"Kirkpatrick? Sure. I dig the Gaelic ones." He gave it a touch of burr.

"Scottish?" Maggie said, surprised. "Somehow I took you for one of us—Irish."

"A little of each-each," McCall said. He glanced at his watch. "Two minutes to go. Want to listen with me, Maggie?"

"No, I've got to run back to the shop. I'll catch it in my car—I parked it on the street, too." She turned away with a businesslike, almost a curt, nod.

He watched her get into a dusty, fender-dented Olds about ten years old and shoot away from the curb like a cop. McCall climbed into the Ford, still smiling. He quickly tuned the radio dial to BOKO's frequency. He turned on his motor, let the engine idle, and snapped the radio switch.

A disk was coming to an end. It was followed by a commercial for a local shlock outfit, a discount clothing store. Then an announcer with the improbable name of Cubbage came on:

"We interrupt the Dave Banner show to bring you a news bulletin to be followed by a special report.

"Black Hearts leader Harlan James failed to appear for the scheduled start of his trial for sedition in district court 2A at the county courthouse this morning. Moments ago the BOKO newsroom learned that the ten-thousand-dollar bail posted to assure the appearance of the Black Hearts leader has been forfeited, and presiding Judge Wendell Graham has issued a bench warrant for Mr. James's arrest.

"Now for the special report:

"At 8:30 this morning a package was delivered to this station by a Negro messenger who left without identifying himself. The package contained a spool of tape for a tape recorder, also a letter signed in ink 'Harlan James.' The letter, typewritten and addressed to 'News Department, Station BOKO,' reads as follows:

" 'Copies of this letter and duplicate tapes have been sent to all area radio and TV stations.

" 'I hereby publicly announce that I will not submit to standing trial in the racist-pig district court of the racist-pig judge Wendell Graham on the phony charge of sedition framed against me by the racist-pig district attorney Volper.

" 'I have gone underground to protect myself. However, I plan to remain in the Banbury general area.

" 'I wish it absolutely understood that none of my blood-relatives, including the sister at whose home I have been living, nor any brother of the Black Hearts organization, including our officers, knows where I am. I am purposely keeping my hideout secret from them so as to prevent their being harassed by the racist-pig police in attempts to make them reveal my whereabouts. They do not know it.

" 'The accompanying tape contains a message to my black brothers and sisters which I demand you play over the air. I will send you further tapes, provided this one is played by you, as a means of keeping in touch with my people who believe in me.

" 'I have no real hope that any of the stations to which I am sending these tapes will play them over the air, because the radio and TV stations of the Banbury area have too often demonstrated their racist, anti-black bias. If you do play them, why not? If you do not play them—why?

" 'From the bottom of my black heart, Harlan James.' "

The newscaster went on:

"In spite of its inflammatory nature, station BOKO has decided to play Harlan James's tape over the air. Our decision stems from BOKO's conviction that the public, white and black, has the right—indeed, the civic obligation—to hear from his own lips just what kind of man James is, and what kind of violent revolutionary doctrine he is preaching. We believe that this taped message, far from winning James converts to his cause—which is evidently his reason for sending it to us—will alert all decent law-abiding citizens to the danger posed by the message and the man.

"The next voice you hear will be that of Harlan James, on the tape he has had delivered to us, complete except for certain obscenities which cannot, of course, be broadcast and which our technicians have blipped out."

There was a pause. Then a resonant bass voice said, "My black brothers and sisters, greetings from the bottom of my black heart. This is Harlan James, president of the Black Hearts, speaking."

21

The fifteen-minute harangue that followed seemed to McCall feeble stuff. It was the familiar catalogue of grievances against "honky" mistreatment of the black man, all true enough, and a bitter exhortation to blacks to "stand up and fight" for their rights. The language was liberally spattered with blips; but nothing in James's speech advocated violent revolution, as the announcer Cubbage had implied; if there was anything subversive in James's message, it eluded McCall. His chief objections to it were that there was nothing new in it, that it was often disjointed and hard to follow, and that the leaders of other black militant movements had said the same things with far greater clarity and imagination.

A typical passage went: "The day when black men could be dismissed as 'niggers' by Mr. Charlie is gone for all time. Now the black man walks down the middle of the sidewalk, and let the honky step out of his way! Now we don't turn the other cheek when we're hit; we hit back twice as hard! When Whitey uses a broom handle on you, use a baseball bat on him. Whitey pulls a pistol on you, you blast him with both barrels of a shotgun before he can pull the trigger. My black brothers and sisters, you want to break the chains of slavery? Don't you ever back one inch away from a honky threat."

You would have to be a white supremacist to interpret this as outright advocacy of violence, McCall thought. If a white man were to advocate the same tactics against threatening blacks, it would be construed in the dominant society as permissible self-defense.

James's recitation of abuses and oppressions had been voiced ten thousand times by blacks and whites alike. The clichés of "honky," "slavemaster," "racist pig," "exploiter," "oppressor" were all there. Even the blipped words could be identified, by the context in which they were used, as the sterile obscenities employed for now

22

worn out shock value by radical groups, both black and white.

There were no solutions presented. Stand your ground. Fight back. Spit in Whitey's eye. As if mere defiance were an end in itself. It was the static philosophy of anger, offering nothing but the satisfaction of manhood.

Maybe, McCall thought, that's enough for a black man who's been molded into something less than a man by the forces of white society. Maybe it's a necessary step in the evolution of a truly integrated community. But it certainly offered little hope for a peaceful today or tomorrow.

For all its lack of creativeness, Harlan James's speech pulsed with power. The man was a natural mover of people, intense, emotional, personally magnetic. It was easy to understand, after listening to his delivery, how James had gathered the loyal following of his Black Hearts.

McCall sat thoughtfully for a few moments when the tape ended. Then he headed for the city hall.

THREE

No one was in the reception room at Mayor Potter's office at city hall but the receptionist.

She was enough.

All his life—at least as far back as he could remember—McCall had had a thing about auburn hair. It was curious, because his mother had been a blonde, and he could recall no significant female in his childhood, teachers included, with hair of the shade that never failed to turn him on. Perhaps it came from a forgotten trip to a museum and the memory of a Titian painting, although there was a subtle difference between the hair color called titian—brownish orange—and the reddish brown of auburn. However it had started, he had never seen a girl with auburn hair whom he had not thought attractive, no matter how plain her features. The phenomenon was one of his life's minor mysteries, like a passion for haggis.

The girl at the reception desk had true auburn hair, painted by nature, not chemistry. Even without the auburn hair she would have attracted him: sea-green eyes, the flawless pale complexion, a chest development that the U.S. Marine Corps would call "outstanding."

At the moment he first caught sight of her, her hands lay below the level of her desktop.

McCall said: "May I see your left hand?"

The girl looked up, startled. "I beg your pardon?" Her voice went along with the rest of her—in the alto range, a touch on the husky side, uncorrupted by provincial inflection.

"Your left hand—please. I'd very much like to see it."

She raised her hands, looking at them, puzzled.

"Thank God!" McCall said, and advanced. "My name is Mike McCall. You're Mayor Potter's secretary?"

"That's right. Also his receptionist and errand girl. The mayor's even been known to weep on my shoulder."

"He's no fool, at his age or half of it." McCall surveyed her with pleasure. "I'd love to know your name."

"Laurel Tate."

"Laurel Tate," he repeated, like a gourmet sampling a delectable new recipe.

The girl looked at her left hand again, frowning. Suddenly she threw back her head and laughed. "*Mister* McCall. It would serve you right if I told you I always leave my wedding ring home."

"Do you?"

"No, that's why I can't honestly tell it to you. I don't have a wedding ring."

"Because you're not married?"

"That's the usual reason."

"I don't know. Things change fast these days. Anyway, I wanted to be sure."

"Mr. McCall, I'd just adore listening to more of your line," Laurel Tate said, "but I have work to do for my boss, so I'm going to have to ask what I can do for you. And don't give me the usual answer!" she added hastily. "I didn't mean it that way."

McCall went over and rested one buttock on the corner of her desk. "I can't seem to remember why I'm here."

"You're Irish, aren't you?" Her smile was blinding. He had never seen such beautiful teeth.

"Half. The other half's Scottish."

"Thank goodness the blarney part is only fifty percent! With the full hundred you'd be a menace to public health. Obviously, Mr. McCall, you came here to see the

25

mayor . . . McCall," she said suddenly. "Didn't you say *Mike* McCall? Mike McCall! Are you *the* . . . ?"

"I'm *the.*"

"Oh." Her pale cheeks had turned coral pink. "I'm so sorry, Mr. McCall! If I'd had any idea . . . The mayor's in conference just now, but I don't think he'll be more than a few minutes more . . . Please have a seat."

"Could you make it Mike?"

The coral deepened. "I don't really think—"

"Mike, or I'll tell the governor on you."

"Don't do that—Mike—I need my job." She had a dimple, too. "But please, not in front of the mayor. He's old-fashioned about his secretaries."

"All right, just when we're alone. By the way, is half past six too early for you?"

"Too early for what?"

"Dinner. To pick you up."

"Are you sure you're Governor Holland's Mike McCall?" Laurel demanded. "You sound more like an advance man for a white slave ring."

"You haven't answered my question."

"I could say this is so sudden."

"It is. But it's a sudden age. I'm tearing down the straightaway at top speed to cover as much territory as I can before some kook drops the bomb. Don't tell me, Laurel, you're going to act coy."

She laughed again. "Six-thirty will be fine. How do you want me to dress?"

"Something simple. I'm a simple man. Where do I find you?"

She typed rapidly on a sheet of scratch paper: *Apt. 2C, 3217 Ralston Road, 884-1796.* McCall pocketed it and, nodding, headed for one of the chairs lined up against the far wall. He had scarcely seated himself when three men filed gloomily out of the inner office and left.

Laurel snapped a lever on her intercom. "Mr. McCall from the capital is here, Mr. Mayor."

A high and hearty voice shouted, "Send him in!"

Heywood Potter was waiting before his big oval desk when McCall entered the mayoral sanctum. The mayor was a Humpty-Dumpty sort of man who looked barely seventy, let alone eighty-four. His chubby, almost un-wrinkled face was topped by a knoll of deep snow; tufted brows slanted upward like horns. Only his shrewd blue eyes betrayed him—they were bloodshot, rheumy, very tired-looking.

"Mike!" He shook McCall's hand like a pump handle. "How's Sam?"

"Never better, Mr. Mayor," McCall said. "Sends his best, and said to tell you it was one of the saddest days of his life when he learned you were retiring from politics."

"Nobody goes on forever." The old man trotted around his desk and plumped himself down in the dwarfing swivel chair. "Have a cigar, Mike?"

"I've quit, thanks. But I still enjoy smelling the smoke of the other guy's."

"No point in my quitting," the mayor said, biting off the end of a long green cigar. "Not at my age, after seventy years of addiction. Sit down, Mike, sit down." He used his desk lighter, puffed until he was satisfied, and leaned back. The old eyes looked McCall over. "It's this racc business, isn't it?" he asked abruptly.

"Yes, sir," McCall said. "I assume you've heard about Harlan James not showing up in court this morning?"

Mayor Potter nodded. "I didn't catch the BOKO broadcast, but one of my aides did. I had my staff check the other area radio and TV stations, by the way. They all did receive the same letter and tape this morning, as advertised, only the others got theirs in the mail. BOKO was the only one to rate messenger delivery."

27

"Isn't that odd?"

"Not really, Mike. The trial was scheduled to start at nine A.M. It so happens that the mail delivery schedules for the studios range from nine to ten. James must have wanted at least one station to have the letter and tape before the trial was due to begin, and the only way he could get it there in time was my messenger."

"But why BOKO? Why not one of the TV stations, for example?"

"Because BOKO," the old politico said dryly, "is the only station in this neck of the woods James could be sure would put his immortal words on the air. Don't forget BOKO is owned by Gerry Horton, and anything inflammatory by a black man can only win Horton votes. The fact is, I'm told none of the other stations plan to air the tape. They're just giving résumés of it on their regular newscasts."

"The messenger hasn't been identified?"

The mayor shook his head. "I talked to Chief Condon. Nobody but the station manager, Cordes, saw the messenger. Aside from being positive the man wasn't Harlan James himself, Cordes couldn't give the police much of a description."

"Airing that speech of James's seems to me pretty irresponsible policy," McCall said, "especially the timing. It's bound to increase the tension in town."

"Of course, Mike. As I said, the more race tension, the greater the appeal of Horton's law-and-order pitch to the scared-to-death whites."

"It's a hell of a way to win an election!"

"Political campaigns aren't usually conducted on the highest ethical plateaus," the mayor remarked. "And I doubt if Gerry Horton even knows the meaning of the word. Yes, Laurel?"

The auburn-haired lovely's alto came over the intercom: "Mr. Cunningham is on line one, Mr. Mayor.] says it's important."

"Excuse me, Mike." The old man picked up one of his three phones and punched a button. "Yes, Marsh?"

His cottony brows came together in a frown as he listened. After a moment he took the cigar out of his mouth and barked, "If we had any doubts about the D.A.'s motives, this pretty well kicks them in the pants. Volper wants a riot, all right. . . . Oh? No, he wouldn't listen to me. But Mike McCall's in my office, and maybe he can do something. Thanks, Marsh."

Mayor Potter banged the phone and flipped his cigar ash angrily in the general direction of the tray. "That was one of my staff. He just got word our eager-beaver D.A.'s engineered a warrant for LeRoy Rawlings's arrest on a conspiracy charge. This could do it, damn him."

"Rawlings?" McCall searched his memory. Then he recalled where he had heard the name. Harlan James's lawyer, Wade, had referred to LeRoy Rawlings as vice president of the Black Hearts and James's closest friend.

"Conspiracy to do what?" McCall demanded.

"To aid a fugitive felon."

"On what ground?"

The mayor shook his head. "Volper claims he has evidence that Rawlings not only knows where James is, he set up his hideout."

"James's letter to BOKO said that no Black Hearts member knows where he is."

"James is hardly a disinterested party. He would naturally want to protect his membership. Anyway, Volper chooses not to believe him. I hardly believe him myself."

"Do you suppose the D.A. really has evidence of Rawlings's complicity?"

"I doubt it," the old man said dryly. "I think Volper's game is to give the black community something to raise

29

hell about, now that James has gone underground and removed their reason for rioting about *him*. Yes, sir, that's what I think."

"Nice town you've got here, Mr. Mayor." McCall rose. "I do believe I'll amble on over to police headquarters. What kind of reception do you expect I'll get there?"

"Distant, my boy. Oh, you'll just love my chief of police. If I didn't regularly sit on Jay Condon, he'd be running nightly patrols through the west side whooping it up with riot guns and tear gas."

"Seems to me Banbury's biggest problem is its law enforcement personnel."

Mayor Potter spat out a shred of tobacco. "Why do you think I'm retiring?"

Governor Holland had chuckled that Heywood Potter's reason for quitting the political arena was that he wanted more time to cultivate the boudoir. Since his wife's death, the octogenarian had been seen around town hitting the night spots with highly attractive lady companions—mature ones, to be sure, but even those half his age were in that category. The gossip was that His Honor was enjoying a second juvenescence; the late Mrs. Potter had hardly been the type, either physically or psychologically, to nourish a man's libido. Looking down on the vigorous man in the big chair, McCall could well believe it.

He grinned, waved, and walked out—to the beauteous Miss Laurel Tate, whose selection as the mayor's secretary seemed suddenly to have taken on added meaning.

Then McCall felt ashamed of himself, kissed the top of Miss Tate's startled auburn locks *en passant*, said, "Remember, six-thirty," and left.

FOUR

It was past eleven, and McCall decided to get himself settled before visiting police headquarters. He chose the Banbury Plaza. It was in the heart of the downtown district, within a short distance of the county courthouse, the city hall, and police headquarters.

Because his work for Governor Holland had him on the road living in hotels or motels much of the time, McCall had developed a hearty distaste for the usual bedroom accommodation. He checked into a two-room suite that had a bar and a refrigerator in the sitting room.

By the time he had settled in, showered, and changed his clothes, it was half past noon. He lunched in the Revolutionary Room (they were thinking of a different revolution, he grinned to himself, when they planned its red, white, and blue décor) on mediocre steak and kidney pie, fortified himself with a couple of digestive tablets against the almost certain future, and got to the police building at 1:15.

Police headquarters occupied a square redstone of four stories, circa 1915, full of stone curlicues and chipped gilt. The lobby was narrow, high-ceilinged and dirty-tiled. An arch to the right announced itself in gilt as CENTRAL DISTRICT. The left displayed a long counter and a single door. The sign over the door said PRESS ROOM. The sign over the counter advertised INFORMATION. An officer in uniform presided behind the counter; he was reading a copy of *Playboy* concealed under an afternoon newspaper.

Directly ahead of McCall, at the end of the lobby, were the elevators.

It seemed a shame to disturb the officer at the information counter, so McCall walked down the lobby and consulted the building directory between the elevators. He took one of the elevators to the fourth floor.

The door to 401 was open, and McCall walked in. There was a long counter, and facing the counter there was a long bench, totally unoccupied. On the other side of the counter a door announced in the universal chipped gilt lettering: CHIEF OF POLICE.

Behind the counter sat a desk, a typewriter on a stand, a number of filing cabinets, and a woman. The woman was wearing a blue police uniform; she was typing. At McCall's entry she looked up, rose, and came over to the counter.

His first thought was that Banbury's bureaucrats had a remarkably discriminating taste in secretaries. His second was that her hair was the exact blonde shade of his mother's (O Freud, O Adler!). But everything else about this one was different. Her eyes were a warm blue-violet (his mother's had been a rather cold sea-water gray). Her build, what he could detect of it under the police uniform, was substantial, even generous, in all the prescribed places, and rugged-looking in a feminine way. An athletic chick, no doubt of it. Confirmed by the deep tan, which went so attractively with the very light hair. She probably swam like a dolphin, rode like a cowgirl, and went around the golf course in the low eighties.

She was also, McCall noted with deep disappointment, untouchable, at least in his book, which dot-dot-dotted any pursuit of women attached to other men by legal ties. She was wearing both a diamond and a wedding ring. And she was returning his inspection with amusement.

"At first I thought you were a vacuum cleaner salesman," the lady policeman said, "I mean from the way you were giving me the twice-over. But now I realize you're strictly in the amateur class. Didn't you notice that the rings are on my right hand, not the left?"

"I beg your pardon," McCall said. "I didn't realize I was being so obvious about it. I'm not usually. As for the rings, I was just about arriving at the correct conclusion." Which undoubtedly was that she was a widow, but he did not explicate. He was feeling too good about the whole thing.

She colored; he had probably offended her. He rather liked that. "Yes, sir?" she said.

He showed her his shield case. The blush enlarged and spread into territory he could not see. "Oh," she said faintly. "I *am* sorry. I don't know what you must . . ." She broke off and tossed her head. "I'm *not* sorry! I suppose I shouldn't be so touchy, Mr. McCall, but there are certain looks men give me that send me absolutely up the wall!"

"And very properly, too," McCall said. "I apologize again. But it's something of a shock to run into somebody like you in a police uniform. Let's pretend it never happened, shall we?"

"All right," she said. And she smiled, and he smiled back. "I suppose you want to see Chief Condon, Mr. McCall. He isn't back from lunch yet. I expect him any minute, though, if you don't mind waiting."

"I'll wait," McCall said. "Meanwhile, maybe you can tell me: has LeRoy Rawlings been picked up yet?"

"A few minutes ago. The chief asked Communications to keep him posted, and they just phoned that a detective team radioed in that they'd made the collar."

"Then you don't know if they've actually brought him in?"

"I doubt if there's been time."

"Where will Rawlings be taken?"

"Depends on whether they decide to book him first, or

33

question him. Arrests are booked in central district, on the main floor. They'll probably question him in the detective bureau. That's on the second floor."

"Thank you, Officer." He shook his head. "I just can't get used to calling such a female-looking female 'officer.'"

Her blonde lashes swept her cheeks. "I loathe it myself. The only thing I loathe more is to be called Fuzzy. My name is Beth McKenna."

"Another Irisher?" McCall shook his head. "Two-thirds of the women in this town seem to be Irish."

"Off base again," Policewoman Beth McKenna said with a giggle. "My maiden name was Svensen. My late husband was the Irishman."

"Late? I'm sorry." So he had been right.

"It was five years ago and the wound's sort of healed," she said lightly. "I can even talk about it now. He was a police lieutenant and he walked into a liquor store holdup while he was off duty. He and the bandit shot together, and they killed each other. And that was that."

"You couldn't have been married long."

"Seven months."

McCall shook his head. "I don't want to keep you from your work. I'll sit down over there—"

"You're not keeping me from anything, Mr. McCall."

"Would it offend you if I asked you to make it Mike?"

"Offend me? Heavens, no! I call half the men in the department by their Christian names."

Just in case I had any ideas, McCall grinned to himself. He liked her more and more.

"If you hate 'officer,' what shall I call you?"

"That shouldn't be much of a problem," she said; she had a dimple, too! "I've just told you my name."

"Mrs. McKenna, or Beth?"

"Depends."

"On what?"

She looked at him very steadily. "Make it Beth," she

34

said suddenly. "Incidentally, two-thirds of the women in this town are *not* Irish. About forty percent are Polish, Italian, or Bohemian, and maybe twenty-five percent are black. Where did you get your statistics?"

"Personal investigation. So far I've met three women, including you. One of the other two was a Maggie Kirkpatrick." And the other one, he thought, Laurel Tate, I made a date with for tonight. Maybe I made a mistake . . .

"The newspaperwoman?"

"Yes."

"Oh." It was a most equivocal "oh." "She's very nice."

"That sounds like the kiss of death."

"Oh, no! I meant it."

"I bet. What's wrong with her?"

"Did I say anything was wrong with Miss Kirkpatrick?"

"Of course you did."

"Well, I didn't. I said she's very nice, and she is."

It went that way for the fifteen minutes more that elapsed before Chief of Police Condon returned from his lunch. And just before the chief's entrance McCall proposed, and Policewoman Beth McKenna accepted, a dinner date for the following evening.

Chief Condon was a leather-tough, ramrod-backed citizen in his late fifties with a grim eye and a belligerent jaw. There was not a gray hair in his head. McCall was willing to bet that he could still take on any man in his department, regardless of youth.

Policewoman McKenna introduced McCall, and informed the chief of the call from Communications. Condon grunted acknowledgment of LeRoy Rawlings's arrest, offered McCall a regulation handshake, and pointedly led the way into his private office.

The office was larger than the mayor's, and contained a larger desk. McCall hoped silently that this contrast did not reflect the relative importance the modern American attached to policing his community and governing it.

"Sit down, Mr. McCall," the chief said. His high-backed swivel was bigger than Mayor Potter's, too. And it was leather, not a synthetic. "What can I do for you?"

"For Governor Holland, Chief. I'm just his errand boy."

"A lot more than that, from what I hear," Condon said dryly. "Look, Mr. McCall, I'm not going to debate you on the law-and-order issue, or blacks versus whites. Tell me what you want."

"Fair enough," McCall said. "Are there any leads yet to that messenger who delivered the tape and letter to BOKO?"

Condon shook his head. "He walked into the station manager's office, laid it on the desk, and walked out without a word. No one else saw him, and he was gone before the manager, a man named Ben Cordes, opened the package. The manager estimates the man's height as five ten to six feet and his weight as between 170 and 190. But he could give no further description except that the messenger was a dark Negro. Says all blacks look alike to him."

"Then how did he know it wasn't Harlan James himself?"

"James has been on TV enough so that Cordes would have recognized him, he says." The glacial eyes bored into McCall's. "But you can't be in Banbury about this James business, McCall. What's the governor hot and bothered about?"

"He's worried about possible race trouble, Chief Condon."

The chief said coldly, "We're capable of maintaining law and order without interference from the capital."

36

McCall's smile said, "Of course." Aloud, he said, "You don't think there's any danger of violence, then?"

"Some of the uppity blacks may try to start something. I don't plan to let it develop past the attempt-to-incite stage."

"Oh? What's your plan to avert it?"

"Good old-fashioned riot control, McCall," the chief drawled. "Whatever force is necessary to maintain or restore order."

"Tear gas? Riot guns?" McCall asked with the same smile. "Mace?"

"Sure. If necessary."

McCall slid down in the chair with his feet stretched out before him. "Have you read the report of the President's Commission on Violence, Chief?"

"I read news accounts of it."

"Then you might have missed the part where they suggest that curing the causes of unrest among minority groups was a more sensible approach to riot prevention than the knee-jerk reaction of meeting mob violence with police violence. Of course, from a long-range point of view, this will involve solving the tough problems of poverty and rotting slums, but the Commission pointed out that riots are often touched off by avoidable incidents. Arresting LeRoy Rawlings on this conspiracy charge, for instance. Do you really have any evidence that Rawlings helped Harlan James go underground?"

"I didn't obtain the warrant, McCall," Chief Condon snapped. "District Attorney Volper did. Ask him what his evidence is. For your information, the function of police is to collect and preserve evidence for the district attorney's use, and to make necessary arrests. It's not up to us to pass on the validity of evidence. It's the district attorney's job to judge whether evidence is sufficient to ask for an indictment or to file information."

37

"I have a degree in law, Chief," McCall said dryly. "I'm quite aware of the constitutional limits placed on the police. But another role of the police, too often neglected, is to prevent crime. In that role you have every legal right to demand of the district attorney just what evidence he has for ordering this arrest, on the grounds of its possible incitement to public disorder. That one simple move on your part might keep a lot of people from getting killed."

In an iceberg voice the police chief said, "We run this city by our rules, McCall, not Sam Holland's. You can tell the governor that we appreciate his interest in Banbury but we don't need his advice."

McCall looked at Condon for several seconds. Then he pulled his legs up and got to his feet. "I'll tell the governor what you said, of course, Chief. But I suggest you keep his phone number handy. You may need it one of these nights."

"That'll be the day. *Or* night." The briefest smile lifted the corners of Condon's lips. But then he said, "What for?"

"To ask him to call out the National Guard. Nice meeting you, Chief. You're everything I've heard." And McCall gave Condon a friendly smile and wave and walked out. Policewoman Beth McKenna looked quickly at him as he left the chief's office, and he raised his eyes heavenward and left.

But then he stuck his head back in. "Remember," he said. "Tomorrow night."

Isn't this where I came in? he thought.

FIVE

McCall took the elevator to the second floor. The detective bureau was directly across the hall from where he stepped out. An arch took him into a long hall that ended at the door to the bureau's squadroom. On the left side of the hall stood a counter behind which sat a uniformed sergeant, male this time. A door across the hall was gilt-lettered CHIEF OF DETECTIVES.

McCall flashed his gold shield, dazzled the sergeant, and asked if LeRoy Rawlings had been brought in yet.

"No, sir. Unless they took him to central district for booking first. Want me to check?"

"Please."

The sergeant called downstairs and was informed that the Black Hearts vice president had not yet been brought in. He left word for the arresting officers to notify the detective bureau if they did show up at central district.

"Now we'll catch them no matter where they check in, Mr. McCall. By the way, Mrs. Franks is here. Another team brought *her* in."

"Who's Mrs. Franks?"

"Isobel Franks, Harlan James's sister. He lives with her, or did until he jumped bail. She's a widow a good fifteen years older than he is. She took him in after their father and mother died, when he was a teenager. He's not married."

"Mrs. Franks is in there?" McCall nodded at the squadroom door.

"Yes, sir. With Sergeant Dixon and Officer Spera."

The squadroom was a huge room full of plain tables

39

and chairs. There were three phones to a table, one at each end and one in the middle.

Four men in plainclothes sat at different tables, two using phones, two studying file folders. Another pair were in a corner with a middle-aged black woman, thin and bitter-mouthed. One of the men sat on the edge of a table, swinging a foot. The other sat beside the woman. They were neither talking to nor looking at her. Just sitting. McCall knew the technique. He felt himself bridle, and made a conscious effort to control himself.

He went over and produced his shield case. The man seated on the table edge was big, blond, bullnecked. His partner was small and swarthy, with liquid Latin eyes. It was not difficult to decide which was Sergeant Dixon and which Officer Spera.

The big blond man grunted. "So?" he said.

Sergeant Dixon's tone was deliberately insolent, even provocative. So the word's gone out already, McCall thought. The governor's boy is snooping around, and give him the back of your hand.

"So this," McCall said. He indicated the rigid black woman in the chair. "What's the story on this lady?"

"Her?" Sergeant Dixon said, and from the way he said it McCall could have smashed his mouth. "She's James's sister."

"I'm aware of that. I mean why is she here?"

"The D.A. wanted her picked up. He's supposed to be along any minute."

"What's the charge?"

"No charge," the blond man drawled. "He just wants to talk to her."

The thin black woman said in a toneless voice, "I have nothing to say to Pig Volper. For the tenth time, I want to phone my lawyer."

McCall looked from the sergeant to his partner. "Are you two preventing this lady from calling her lawyer?"

"She's not a suspect," Officer Spera said. He had a surprisingly deep voice. "The Supreme Court never said anything about witnesses who aren't charged with anything having the right to counsel. You want us to start giving their rights to every holdup witness we talk to?"

"Mrs. Franks isn't a holdup witness. The D.A. undoubtedly wants to ask her where her brother is, and her answer might well be self-incriminating. So she definitely has a right to legal advice. Why are you withholding that right?"

"Because Art Volper would skin us alive if we didn't," Sergeant Dixon said with a grin. "Next question, Mr. McCall?"

McCall heard the squadroom door open and glanced around. Two detectives, white, were bringing a black man into the room. One of the detectives was tall and lanky and had a sad look on his bony face. The other was short and burly and harried-looking. The man between them was a six-footer, lean, very black-skinned, with an Afro hair style. All three were thirtyish.

It struck McCall that the black man answered the vague description of the messenger provided by BOKO's station manager.

The detectives led their man to the corner. The black man looked down at the black woman and said, "They got you, too, huh, Issy?"

"Hello, Roy," she said. "They won't let me call Mr. Prentiss Wade."

"Me, either." LeRoy Rawlings looked around the circle of white faces. He added casually, "What do you expect of pigs?"

He uttered the invective without venom, as if it were a ritual expected of him. It brought a glare from the blond Dixon, and Spera jumped to his feet.

Neither of the detectives who had brought the prisoner in seemed disturbed. The lanky one with the

41

mournful expression said in a bored tone, "Oh, sit down, Spera. Aren't you used to this stuff yet?"

Spera slowly reseated himself. The lanky detective looked at Isobel Franks. "Who's she?"

"Harlan James's sister," Sergeant Dixon said.

The man stared. "Did Volper blow a fuse?"

Dixon shrugged. "I just work here, Lieutenant. He said bring her in, we brought her in."

The lanky man shook his head and turned his attention to McCall. "The desk man said you wanted to see us, Mr. McCall. I'm Lieutenant Cox, my partner here is Sergeant Fenner."

He offered his hand; his stocky partner followed suit. The handshakes were friendly. So not all the Banbury police danced to Chief Condon's tune. Or maybe, McCall thought, they hadn't heard the music yet.

McCall nodded toward LeRoy Rawlings. "What's the story on this man, Lieutenant?"

"Maybe we'd better discuss it in private, Mr. McCall. Dixon, keep an eye on him a minute, will you?" He led the way to the opposite corner. His partner came along, too. Lieutenant Cox eyed McCall with what seemed to be a chronic dyspepsia.

"Mind telling us your mission in Banbury, Mr. McCall? Or is it confidential?"

McCall shook his head. "No secret. The governor is worried about possible race trouble. He sent me to try to head it off."

The lieutenant nodded. "I was hoping that was why you're here. Maybe you can talk some sense into District Attorney Volper. This arrest of LeRoy Rawlings is stupid. The black community's going to blow when they hear about James's sister being pulled in."

"She's not under arrest, Dixon told me," McCall said. "The D.A. merely wants to question her."

"That's something, anyway. Except Volper'd be quite

42

capable of tossing her in the can if he decides she knows where her brother is."

"Then we get to see Chief Condon's theories about riot control put into effect," Sergeant Fenner grumbled. "Because the lid will shoot right off the west end."

"West end, Sergeant? Is that the ghetto area?"

Fenner nodded. "Also known as Blacktown. By the same people who say 'nigger.'"

The squadroom door opened again, this time imperiously; the plump, pink man with the gray crewcut and the eyes of a slug whom McCall had seen at the prosecution table in the courtroom that morning came in. District Attorney Volper beat them to the occupied corner by a step.

He glanced at McCall, apparently assumed he was a new member of the detective bureau, and dismissed him. McCall could have pushed his face in.

He said abruptly to Lieutenant Cox, "You get anything out of Rawlings?"

"We haven't asked him anything, Mr. Volper," Cox said. "We just brought him in."

Volper stared at Dixon, who had risen and was standing like a soldier. "Get anything out of her?"

Sergeant Dixon said, "We kind of figured you'd want to question this one personally, Mr. Volper."

The D.A. nodded his approval. He turned his wet eyes to Isobel Franks. "Do you know where your brother is, Mrs. Franks?"

"You don't have to answer any pig question, Issy," LeRoy Rawlings said. "Look here, Volper. I demand my right to phone my attorney, Mr. Wade."

"You shut up till I get to you."

"You forgot to say 'boy,'" Rawlings said.

Something like life crept into the dead eyes. "One more comment like that out of you, Rawlings, and I'll have you dragged out of here and tossed in a cell!"

"And beat up?"

"I guess we better oblige him, Mr. Volper," the big blond sergeant said with a grin.

"Shut up!" the district attorney said. "Rawlings, you going to keep your mouth shut?"

Before the black man could reply, Mrs. Franks said, "Roy. Please. Don't get yourself dragged away. I'd like you to be here."

"Sure, Issy. Just for you, I won't call this pig a pig any more."

Volper chose to ignore this.

"You haven't answered my question, Mrs. Franks!"

She shook her head. "I'm not answering no questions, no, sir. Not till I've talked to Mr. Prentiss Wade."

"But you're not under arrest!"

"Then what am I doing here?" she asked quietly. "I didn't want to come. They made me."

"Next thing you know she'll say we slapped her around," Sergeant Dixon said. "Right, Issy?"

"My name is Mrs. Franks!" she flashed at him.

"Dixon, what did I tell you?" The district attorney's pink was now in the red range. "Mrs. Franks, do you know that aiding and abetting a person under indictment to jump bail is a felony in this state when the bail is more than a thousand dollars?"

"Pardon me," McCall said. "That law hasn't been invoked since it went into the book. You might conceivably stick Mrs. Franks with the same charge you're bringing against Mr. Rawlings here, if you can prove she helped arrange her brother's flight, but anything else would be reaching for it, wouldn't you agree, Mr. District Attorney?"

Volper had wheeled to stare at him as if he had turned into a man-sized bullfrog. "Who the hell are you?"

Lieutenant Cox coughed. "This is Mr. McCall, Governor Holland's special assistant, Mr. Volper."

Volper blinked. After a moment he growled, "I thought you were one of the bureau officers. Still, I don't think I need any advice about the law, Mr. McCall."

"Seems to me you could use some," McCall said mildly. "The Supreme Court has made it quite clear that arrested persons are entitled to legal counsel from the moment of arrest, before being questioned, unless they knowingly waive. Your prisoner just demanded permission to call his lawyer, and your response was to tell him to shut up. You've already laid the ground for reversal of any conviction you may get against him, Mr. Volper."

Volper started to puff up. "You sound like a lawyer."

"I am."

"Oh? Which bar?"

"Illinois."

"I see." Volper seemed to be considering his options. Finally he said, "As it happens, I haven't asked Mr. Rawlings anything yet, so his constitutional rights haven't been violated. And Mrs. Franks, as you heard me tell her, isn't under arrest."

McCall shrugged. "I could give you an argument about her right to a lawyer, too, but it's your bailiwick, Mr. Volper. I hope you won't mind my observing?"

Volper's expression suggested that he minded very much. At this moment a little half-bald man wearing oversized horn eyeglasses stuck his head timidly into the squadroom. At sight of District Attorney Volper he looked relieved and hurried over. He had the look of a minor executive, and McCall put him down as ten years younger than he looked, which was fiftyish.

"I hurried fast as I could, Mr. Volper," he panted, trotting up. "I mean after I got your message."

"Oh, Mr. Cordes," the district attorney said. "Thanks for coming. Though I did expect you sooner."

"I was out of the studio when you phoned—didn't get

back till just now." His look of worry deepened. "What did you want me for?"

The little man was a floor-starer, and McCall almost expected Volper to take him by the chin and jerk his head up. But all Volper said was, "Do you recognize anyone here, Mr. Cordes?"

The newcomer wrenched his gaze from his study of the floor and looked uneasily from face to face. When he reached the face of LeRoy Rawlings, he drew back, a startled movement. "He's the one," he quavered. "He's the one!"

"The one who, Mr. Cordes?"

"The messenger who delivered the package from Harlan James!"

"You're sure of that, Mr. Cordes?"

"Oh, yes. Oh, yes!"

"I never saw this honky before in my whole life," LeRoy Rawlings said.

"That was a pretty positive identification, Rawlings," Volper said with a smile. "But I'll tell you what I'll do with you. You tell me where Harlan James is hiding out and I think I can promise you the charge against you will be nullified."

"You know what, pig?" Rawlings said, spitting at Volper's shoe. "Go screw."

SIX

McCall had never witnessed an official identification like this one. A black man was to be identified, and only one black man was present. Apparently the lineup technique was not part of Banbury's law enforcement system.

He decided for the time being to remain in the role of observer.

"You fool, Roy," Mrs. Franks said. "Don't you know you're just playing their game?"

"I'm a man!" Rawlings said.

"You're an idiot."

Volper smiled again. He ordered Lieutenant Cox and Sergeant Fenner to take Rawlings downstairs for booking while he questioned Mrs. Franks.

The little man named Cordes asked uneasily, "You through with me, Art—I mean, Mr. Volper?"

Interesting slip, McCall thought. The BOKO station manager wasn't very bright. Of course he and his boss Gerald Horton would be hand-in-glove with the district attorney.

"For now, Mr. Cordes, for now. I'll require you to appear in court later, of course, as a witness."

"Well, sure." The little man shuffled. "Well. I guess in that case I'll run along."

"You do that," Volper said.

The question was, was Cordes party to a police frame-up, or had his been a genuine identification? It was hard to say. At any rate, it merited following up. McCall raised a hand in a general goodbye and sauntered after Cordes. He managed to catch up with the little man at the elevators.

Cordes glanced around at him self-consciously.

McCall stuck out his hand. "They've got bad manners in there, Mr. Cordes. My name is McCall."

The station manager's handshake was as feeble as McCall had expected it to be.

"Benjamin Cordes is mine, Mr. McCall. Are you with the detective bureau or the district attorney's office?"

"Neither," McCall said. "I work for Governor Holland."

"Oh, *that* McCall! Pleased to meet you, Mr. McCall."

The elevator door on the left slid open. A uniformed officer was in the car. McCall was interested to observe that Cordes attempted no further conversation until the elevator reached the lobby. The little man was visibly relieved when the officer left them.

"It's a funny thing," he confided to McCall. "Ever since I was a boy I've been afraid of policemen. Isn't that silly?"

"Not always," McCall said, and Cordes laughed uncertainly. "By the way, Mr. Cordes," he went on as they strolled toward the street doors, "I understand that, in your description of the messenger who delivered the tape and letter, you were only able to give the police a rough approximation of his height and weight, and his skin, I believe you said, was quite dark. You were also quoted as saying that all black men look alike to you. Or did I get it wrong, Mr. Cordes?"

"Oh, I didn't mean it that way," the station manager said quickly. "Not that way at all! I just meant that it's hard to, well, describe a Negro face. I mean to differentiate it from other Negro faces."

"Why is that?" McCall asked.

"Well, I don't know." Cordes seemed offended. "Anyway, as you saw, I certainly had no trouble recognizing his face when I saw him again just now."

"Then you'd never seen Rawlings before he delivered that tape?"

"No."

They were now abreast of the arch into central district. Lieutenant Cox, Sergeant Fenner, and LeRoy Rawlings were ranged before a counter about twenty feet beyond the arch.

McCall said, "You couldn't be mistaken in your identification?"

"Definitely not, Mr. McCall. I'm positive he was the man."

At the glass-paneled exit, half in and half out of the door, McCall paused. "Suppose it develops, Mr. Cordes, that LeRoy Rawlings comes up with an alibi for this morning? Would you still maintain that he was the man who delivered the letter and tape?"

Cordes began to look suspicious. "I just said I was positive, Mr. McCall. I don't know what the governor's trying to do, but it sounds to me as if he's sent you here to whitewash the black element—"

"That's hardly the word I'd use," McCall said dryly.

"You know what I mean! As for an alibi, I'd be surprised if Rawlings doesn't come up with one. Every time a member of the Black Hearts has a run-in with the law, it turns out he was in the company of a dozen other Black Hearts at the time of the offense. An alibi by LeRoy Rawlings or any other Black Heart wouldn't impress me. No, sir, I'm certain he was the messenger."

McCall held the door for him, and the little radio station manager stepped through with dignity. He was not going to make an easily damaged witness, for all his Milquetoast manner. He possessed a stubbornness, an armature of steel, shared by many small men.

"I'm not in Banbury, by the way, to whitewash—or blacken—anybody. The governor's interest is in seeing the city remain peaceful, whatever the problems."

"Of course, of course, Mr. McCall. Sorry I got mad."

Cordes held out his hand. "I'd sure like to get you on a panel show at BOKO. Would you be interested?"

McCall shook the little thing. "Not right now, Mr. Cordes. I'm still in the observation stage. Pleasure to have met you."

"Same here."

Cordes trotted down the marble steps, waving. McCall stepped back into the building. The trio was still at the booking desk; Rawlings was emptying the contents of his pockets.

McCall went the other way, to the information desk. He asked where he might find a pay phone, and the officer told him that there was "a whole raft of them" outside the press room.

McCall found the booths, but before phoning Maggie Kirkpatrick he glanced into the press room. It was empty.

He looked up the number of the Banbury *Post-Telegram* and dialed it. It took him seven minutes by his watch before he heard her voice.

"You have a wonderful paging system, Maggie. I could have reached de Gaulle in less time."

"I was in what we girls euphemistically call the powder room. One of the guys had to beat on the door. What's up?"

"I'll give you a tip in return for a favor."

"Shoot, Mike," Maggie said promptly.

"LeRoy Rawlings is being booked right now on the charge of aiding a fugitive felon to evade arrest. About ten minutes ago Benjamin Cordes, station manager of BOKO, positively identified Rawlings as the messenger who delivered the tape and letter."

"You're a doll!" Maggie said.

"Wait, there's more. Volper had Harlan James's sister, Mrs. Isobel Franks, brought in for questioning about her brother's whereabouts. So far he hasn't come up with anything either from her or Rawlings but a few insults from Rawlings."

Maggie was apparently taking notes. "Is that it, Mike?"

"That's it. Now for the quid pro quo."

"What can I do for you? And keep it clean."

"I want you to phone Prentiss Wade and pass on to him what I just told you. Don't give him your source of information."

"Volper hasn't let Rawlings use the phone?"

"Nor Mrs. Franks. Will you phone Wade right away?"

"Before I file the story, Mike. Thanks!"

When McCall got back to the lobby, the three men were no longer at the booking counter. McCall glanced toward the elevators just in time to see the door of one close behind Lieutenant Cox and Sergeant Fenner. Rawlings was not with them. Presumably he had been deposited in a detention cell.

McCall found himself heading back toward the city hall and wondered why. He had no reason to seek out Mayor Potter again so soon . . . Laurel Tate. That auburn hair will do it every time, he upbraided himself as he turned right on Grand Avenue, and he drove to his hotel. He was seeing her in the evening, anyway.

The thought made him think of Beth McKenna, Chief Condon's girl Friday; and thinking of her blonde hair made him think of Maggie Kirkpatrick, who was nobody's girl Friday and had black hair besides.

The trouble with you, McCall, McCall told his alter ego in the bathroom mirror, you get hungry too often.

With an effort he shut the girls out and phoned Governor Holland, using the governor's private line. He reported the events of the day in detail.

"Looks as if old Heywood Potter was dead right," Sam Holland said. "The opposition's really trying to stir up race trouble to win support on their law-and-order issue."

"I'm sure that's District Attorney Volper's motive, Governor. Whether or not Gerald Horton is in on the play I can't say yet, although it would make sense that he is. I haven't met either mayoralty candidate yet."

"Well, you stick with it, Mike. You have my backing for anything you have to do to prevent a confrontation there, even if it hurts us politically. Your first consideration is to preserve peace. At any cost."

It was such orders, not his substantial salary, that had long since won Mike McCall's total loyalty. McCall could not have worked for most politicians; his personal code, fashioned out of the rough-and-tumble of Chicago's south side during his boyhood, the hard lessons of the Marine Corps during his young manhood, and his law training at Northwestern, called for absolute honesty in public office. Sam Holland was the rarest of politicians: he refused to compromise his moral principles.

They had met when Holland had been a state senator and McCall a private detective. The case, involving the murder of a fellow-legislator and close friend of Holland's, was badly tangled in skeins of venality; it taught each man the virtue of the other, and they became friends. One of Holland's first acts on winning the governorship was to offer Micah McCall a job as his assistant for confidential affairs—his personal troubleshooter. The very large salary that went with the job came out of Governor Holland's pocket. "I don't want you on the state payroll," the governor had said. "That makes you subject to all sorts of pressure. This way you're accountable to only one man, Mike, me."

The years had knitted them together in a tight weave. Holland had at his elbow an honest man he could trust completely, and McCall had found an honest man he could serve with a clear conscience.

It had been argued about the state that a multimillionaire could afford a moral code that to other politicians would have been a disastrous luxury. To McCall these were fighting words. It was true that Samuel F. Holland could have bathed in his millions. But McCall had done homework on Holland's origins, and the arithmetic checked out: he had been honest and uncompromising as a poor man, too.

McCall stripped down to his shorts, closed the vanes of the blinds, and stretched out on the bed. He had been up at four A.M. in order to catch the early plane, and he was tired. He glanced at his watch: a quarter to three. There was still plenty to do before his date with Laurel. He set his mental alarm clock for four o'clock and was asleep in thirty seconds.

SEVEN

McCall awoke at three minutes to four.

He stretched, wide awake and refreshed. Then he picked up the bedside phone and called police headquarters. He asked for the detective bureau and Lieutenant Cox.

The lieutenant chuckled. "Hank Fenner and I enjoyed the law course you gave our fearless district attorney this afternoon, Mr. McCall."

"What happened after I left?"

"Volper got a big fat nothing out of Mrs. Franks and Rawlings. A little past three that black lawyer Prentiss Wade showed up with habeas corpus writs for both of them. How Wade found out they were in custody is beyond me, because Volper hadn't let either make any phone calls."

"Were they released?" McCall asked, deadpan. Good old Maggie.

"Mrs. Franks was. Volper didn't have any grounds to hold her. Rawlings he hauled up before Municipal Court Judge Edmundson for a preliminary hearing. I don't suppose you know much about our local judges?"

"Very little. I saw District Court Judge Graham in action for a few minutes, and he impressed me as fair, even in the face of provocation. But that's the extent of my knowledge."

"Graham's a good judge, which is why Volper picked Edmundson. Edmundson is a Horton boy and a buddy-buddy of Volper's." The lieutenant did not add the name of Chief Condon, but McCall suspected that the omission derived from discretion rather than lack of knowledge. "Plus Edmundson's a racist. In his court disturbing the peace can get you three months in the city jail if your skin is black. If you're white he'll let you off with a fine."

"Say no more," McCall said. "I know the breed. What happened, Lieutenant?"

"Edmundson remanded Rawlings to jail in lieu of fifty thousand dollars' bond."

"Fifty thousand on a charge like this?"

"And in this case, of course, it means Rawlings would have to raise the full amount personally. Since Harlan James ran out on his ten-grand bail, no bondsman would even accept a phone call from a member of the Black Hearts now."

McCall said fretfully, "This might really trigger something on the west side. Is there a chance Judge Edmundson might reconsider and reduce Rawlings's bail to a reasonable sum if somebody pointed out that his action could avert a riot?"

"Not if the somebody was you or me, Mr. McCall. He treated Prentiss Wade like dirt in that court—wouldn't listen to him at all; Wade's fit to be tied. Oh, Edmundson'd take Volper's recommendation, because it was on the D.A.'s argument that he set this ridiculous bail in the first place. But trouble is what Volper wants. The only other man in Banbury who could influence His Honor is Gerald Horton. You know, our councilman-at-large. And candidate for mayor."

"I know. Think Horton would listen to me?"

"He's smarter than Volper, and a politician . . . I just don't know, Mr. McCall. Maybe. He has an office in city hall, phone number Emerson 3-1000. Just a minute . . . Horton's extension is 123."

"Thanks, Lieutenant. Keep your fingers crossed."

"While I'm at it, I've got two legs, too."

McCall called the city hall number and asked for extension 123. It rang and rang. Finally the switchboard operator said in a bored voice, "Mr. Horton's probably gone home. It's almost four-thirty. 'Most everyone here starts leaving around now."

"Ring the mayor's office, please," McCall said. "I'm Mike McCall."

"Yes, sir!" She knew who he was; he heard it in her changed tone. "I doubt anybody's there, either, sir. But I'll try."

There was no answer. McCall said, "This is an early-to-quit town, isn't it? Do you happen to have Councilman Horton's home phone number, doll?"

"I don't have any special list, Mr. McCall." He could almost see her poking her hairdo. "I know it's in the book, though. On Waxman Drive."

"Thanks."

McCall was about to hang up when the operator said, "Sir?"

"Yes."

"I don't think you'll find Councilman Horton home now. I happen to know his wife is out of town."

McCall stopped thinking of other things. "Mr. Horton doesn't go home when his wife is away?"

"Not for dinner. He usually calls some restaurant for a reservation."

"Did he do that this afternoon?"

"Not through me. But it might have been through one of the other operators."

"Thank you." McCall hung up, wondering if the occupants of city hall, up to and including Mayor Potter, were aware of the freedom with which this particular operator passed out information. The whole town was loose.

There was no Gerald Horton listed in the directory but there were several G. Hortons. One was on Waxman Drive. McCall dialed the number.

No answer.

Perhaps Horton was at his radio station—it was too early for him to be having dinner. McCall consulted the phone book again for BOKO. He was memorizing the phone number when he noticed that the station address was 412 N. Grand. The address of the Banbury Plaza was a low number on Grand. McCall flipped back through the directory and found the listing for the hotel. 325 N. Grand. The radio station was less than a block away.

He brushed his teeth, showered, combed out a cowlick, dressed, and left the suite.

The radio station occupied the upper floor of a two-story building, above a furniture store and a clothing store. The wooden staircase leading to it rose between the two stores.

Inside there was a hall leading to the rear. Illuminated signs designated STUDIOS A, B and C, PRODUCTION, CONTINUITY, CONTROL ROOM. To his left, at the top of the stairs, was a door steel-lettered BENJAMIN CORDES, MGR.

McCall now understood why no one but Cordes had seen the messenger. The man who delivered Harlan James's letter and tape had had to pass no other doors to gain access to the station manager's office.

The door was a little ajar. McCall nudged it wider open and looked in.

It was a roomy office containing a conference table neatly punctuated by leatherette chairs and, catercornered, a large glass-topped desk. Cordes sat behind the desk writing on a pad. There was a visitor's chair opposite.

A tall beefy man wearing slacks and a gaudy sports shirt stood on a stepladder in the corner to McCall's left, working with a screwdriver on a ceiling speaker. He glanced down at McCall and went on working. From his build and features—he had the squashed nose and punch-thickened lips of a prizefighter—McCall guessed that he had once made his livelihood in the ring. He appeared in his late forties or early fifties, which would make him a relative old timer. He looked familiar to McCall.

The little man at the desk looked up. "Oh, Mr. McCall! I didn't hear you. Come in, come in. Didn't expect to see you so soon again."

"I didn't either," McCall said.

"Come in. Sit down—"

"I'm actually looking for Mr. Horton, Mr. Cordes. Is he here?"

"Why, no."

"Any idea where I can find him?"

Cordes glanced at the wall clock. "He's probably on his way home, Mr. McCall. He usually leaves his office at the city hall between four and four-thirty."

"I thought he might have stopped in at the station."

"No, if he'd planned to stop in, Mr. Horton would have been here by now. You haven't seen him, Andy, have you?"

The man on the ladder, who had flaming red hair, shook his head.

"The switchboard operator at city hall seemed to think he wouldn't be going home, Mr. Cordes. She said he usually eats out when his wife's away."

"Oh, yes," Cordes looked distressed. "Wilma is off to Carson Springs, that reducing farm. I'd forgotten. Spends a couple of weeks there twice a year. I doubt Gerry will get home before eight or nine. Can't I help you, Mr. McCall?"

"I doubt it," McCall said. "It's a political matter."

The little man beamed. "I happen to be his campaign manager."

McCall looked at him, astonished. Cordes nodded toward the pad he had been writing on. "His speech for tomorrow night."

"You write his speeches?"

"Rewrite would be more accurate, Mr. McCall. I merely—well—polish Mr. Horton's thoughts. The substance is his, not mine. Our next mayor is nobody's puppet, Mr. McCall. He's a man who knows how to lead, and he'll never shirk a responsibility."

McCall sat down in the visitor's chair. "Frankly, I'm surprised, Mr. Cordes. I'd never have suspected you of being the political type."

Benjamin Cordes frowned. McCall even thought that he swelled a little in the chair behind the desk. The banty-rooster syndrome.

"I'm sorry," McCall said apologetically. "I didn't mean that as a dig, Mr. Cordes. I should have learned long ago never to judge a man by his cover."

"I should hope so." Cordes was clearly offended. "Not that any of us can help how the good Lord made us. There are times," he said a little hesitantly, almost shyly, "when I think of myself as . . . well . . . I suppose we all have our daydreams. What I am, Mr. McCall, is strictly a follower. I don't kid myself that I can ever be anything more. Gerald Horton is different. He's a dynamic, self-confident man with drive and vigor, and he's full of creative political ideas."

"He is?" McCall said, fascinated.

"I can only have the greatest respect and admiration for him, and I'm doing all I can to further his political career. I know that some day Gerald Horton will be a household name far beyond the confines of this city and state. He may well become . . . well!" Cordes looked sheepish. "I'm making a campaign speech."

"Such loyalty, Mr. Cordes," McCall murmured, "just has to be deserved."

EIGHT

"Yes," Cordes said. "Well." He was mollified. "Then perhaps now you'll tell me what you want to see Mr. Horton about?"

"Of course," McCall said. "As his campaign manager, speechwriter, and so on, you must be on familiar terms with how Horton thinks. What I wanted to talk to him about was LeRoy Rawlings. Maybe you could give me some idea of what his reaction might be."

"Reaction to what?"

"After you and I left the detective bureau today, a lawyer showed up with writs of habeas corpus for Rawlings and Mrs. Franks. Volper released Mrs. Franks, but he took Rawlings before Judge Edmundson for a preliminary hearing. Edmundson remanded him to jail in lieu of fifty thousand dollars' bail."

The man Cordes had called Andy had climbed down from his stepladder and come around behind the station manager's desk. There was a panel with a switch and a volume control knob in the desk top. The red-haired man activated the switch.

A burst of sound came from the stereophonic speakers at the other end of the room. "——listening to the Bart Wheeler blast on Station BOKO in Banbury," a rich male voice boomed. "Fourteen-ten on your dial. The time is exactly four fifty-seven."

"Do you have to do that now, Andy?" Cordes snapped.

"Sorry." The man reduced the volume. "I didn't know it was tuned so loud, Ben. It's working all right now."

A commercial came on. The red-haired man flicked it off.

The name and the red-haired man's familiar face triggered McCall's memory suddenly. "You're Andy Whalen," he said.

The man looked pleased. "That's right. How come you remember me? I didn't think anybody remembered me any more."

"I saw you fight Kid Cooley in Chicago. When he was the leading middleweight contender."

The ex-boxer wiggled his jaw. "That's when I got my face made over. The kid had a sock like Marciano. I was too old to try a comeback, but I needed the money."

"You did pretty well for an old man," McCall said with a smile. "You had him on the canvas twice."

"And he got up both times," Whalen said with a grin. "Me, when he put me down in the twelfth, I just laid there."

"This is Mr. McCall, Andy," Cordes said. "Mike McCall, from the capital."

"The governor's muscle? I'm honored you remembered me, Mr. McCall."

Whalen came back around the desk, wiping his hand on his pants. McCall shook hands with him.

"Andy is our chief electrician and general maintenance man," Cordes explained.

"I do for Ben about what you do for the governor, Mr. McCall. Troubleshooter, that's me."

Cordes said gently, "Dan wants you to look at that dead mike in Studio C before you leave for the day, Andy."

"Yeah, Ben, sure." Whalen stuck his hand out again. "Nice to have met you, Mr. McCall."

McCall shook it and waved. The redheaded man folded his stepladder and hurried out with it.

"Not exactly punchy," Cordes said, "but . . ." He did not finish. "Where were we, Mr. McCall?"

"We had Rawlings in jail, with bond fixed at fifty thousand dollars. Since Harlan James skipped, naturally no bondsman will go bail for a member of the Black Hearts."

"You can hardly blame them."

"No, but the black community isn't going to take kindly to the unreasonable bail. If this town is close to a race explosion, this might be the detonator. Your man Horton is the local leader of his political party. He must have some influence with the D.A. I thought he might use it to get Rawlings's bail reduced to some reasonable sum."

Cordes looked unhappy. "The D.A. doesn't fix bail, Mr. McCall."

"I know," McCall said. "But according to my information he recommended the figure that was set. Also, in the opinion of somebody who knows the judge and the D.A. both, Edmundson probably would reduce bail to whatever figure Volper suggested. The D.A. ought to be persuaded to change his mind, Mr. Cordes."

Cordes pursed his precise lips. "A phone call direct to the judge would do it, without Horton's having to use Volper as a middleman. As I mentioned before, Gerry Horton is a strong leader. He pretty well runs the local party."

"You think he'd do it?"

Cordes pulled in his head like an alarmed turtle. "I meant he could make Edmundson change his mind if he wanted to. But I don't think he'd want to. Gerry doesn't believe in coddling these black militants."

"Coddling?" McCall said. "The man is charged with an offense that could get him eighteen months. A white man charged with the same crime would likely be released on his own recognizance. It isn't coddling to offer blacks the same treatment as whites."

"It is when they have a history of jumping bail," the little man said.

McCall stared at him. "One Black Heart jumping bail constitutes a history? Do you belong to any organization, Cordes? The Elks, for instance?"

"I'm a Rotarian."

"If some fellow-member of Rotary were arrested for a crime and jumped his bail, should that bar you from bail if you later got into trouble with the law?"

Cordes sniffed. "The Black Hearts can hardly be equated with Rotary, Mr. McCall. Anyway, you're arguing with the wrong person. You asked me what I thought Gerry Horton's reaction would be, and I told you. Nothing you say to me is going to change Gerry's attitude."

"I suppose not. But off the record, Cordes, and strictly because I'm nosy, how does your attitude compare with his?"

The little man thought this over very carefully. "As I said before, Mr. McCall, I'm a follower. I believe Horton has a big political future, and I mean to devote my energies to furthering it in whatever way I can. I suppose Gerry doesn't need me so much as I need him. I believe in him—I guess you could call it an old-fashioned case of hero worship. Anyway, our relationship precludes me from holding divergent political opinions. So your question really isn't pertinent."

"Just a Banbury Boswell?" McCall smiled. "No opinions of your own?"

"None," Cordes replied, "that I would ever express. To you or anyone else, just so long as Gerald Horton has a use for me."

McCall got to his feet. "Loyalty right or wrong is rare these days, Mr. Cordes," he said. "I hope Horton realizes what a jewel he has."

"Thank you, Mr. McCall," the little man said earnestly.

Back in his hotel suite, McCall dialed Horton's home number again. There was still no answer. After dressing

63

for his dinner date he tried once more, with no success. Cordes's guess as to when Horton would get home was probably correct. There was no point in trying again until eight or nine o'clock.

The 3200 block of Ralston Avenue was an area of modern medium-range apartment houses and small homes. Number 3217 was a two-story brick. No elevator, and the aggregate of mailboxes in the lobby added up to ten units to a floor.

McCall climbed a flight of concrete stairs and sought out 2C. He pressed the bell. The door opened immediately.

Laurel Tate was wearing a sleeveless moderate-mini suitable for anything from a neighborhood tavern to a nightclub. Its pine green matched her eyes and haloed her auburn hair.

Her pale skin pinked at McCall's admiration. After a moment she tossed her shining head. "Well, are you just going to stand out there, Mr. McCall? I don't bite."

"I do," McCall said.

"You'd find me tough chewing, Mr. McChaser," Laurel said sweetly. "As the immortal Miss West said, I like a man who takes his time. But thank you for what I take it was meant as a compliment."

She stood aside, and he stepped into her tiny living room. There was nothing distinctive about it, and he felt a twitch of disappointment. The hair sometimes fooled him. Everything was brand-new and of discount-store quality. But the easy chair looked cosy, the lamp behind it shed a good reading light, and there were books as well as a hifi-radio-TV set. He would know a little more when he had a chance to check out the book titles.

He tried to ignore the fake fireplace with its artificial-log-type gas burner.

"Would you care for a drink?" Laurel asked.

"I can wait," McCall said. "How about you?"

64

"All right. I'll get my things."

She went into what he assumed was her bedroom and closed the door behind her. McCall homed in on the bookcase. He immediately felt better. Sociology and psychology textbooks, several volumes on the Peace Corps, a sprinkling of fiction—Malamud, Cheever, *The Ugly American*, an old copy of Kuprin's *Yama: The Pit*; a wide-ranging selection. The lack of distinction in her apartment was probably the result of economics, not taste. She must have bought it all on the installment plan.

Laurel returned carrying a black velvet cape and a matching bag; the evening was too cool for bare arms. She handed McCall the cape with a natural gesture, as if she had been brought up to expect the traditional courtesies. He draped it about her shoulders with the feeling that it was going to be a warm and satisfying evening.

He could not help thinking of Chief Condon's secretary as he handed Laurel into his car. Laurel was all woman. So was Policewoman Beth McKenna, but he suspected that Policewoman McKenna would have emerged from her bedroom with the cape already in place.

NINE

The desk clerk, who apparently felt no particular loyalty to the Banbury Plaza's Revolutionary Room, had recommended the Capri Club's food as the best in town. On the way McCall told Laurel about LeRoy Rawlings's arrest and the outrageously high bail set by Judge Edmundson.

Her first reaction was indignation, but then she looked puzzled. "How does a municipal court judge take jurisdiction in a case involving a felony? I thought such courts handle only misdemeanors."

McCall explained that a writ of habeas corpus required that the person in custody either be released immediately or be brought at once before the nearest available magistrate.

"The term 'nearest available' gives the official on whom the writ is served considerable latitude. What it amounts to is that he can pretty well choose the judge. And all magistrates, of course, have the authority to preside over preliminary hearings and fix bail. The trial itself will be held in district court, and once Rawlings is arraigned the district court judge can reduce the bail if he wants to. But by the time a grand jury acts, or the D.A. gets around to filing an information—whichever route he chooses to go—Rawlings may have been in jail for a month or more."

At the Capri Club, which was already filling up, the maître-d'hôtel took one look at McCall, snapped his fingers for a cocktail waitress, and placed them at a corner table marked RESERVED. By which McCall knew that the Banbury Plaza desk clerk was a steerer for the club.

Laurel ordered a vodka martini. McCall, whose reputation as a hard drinker was wholly undeserved—his job sometimes called for heavy social drinking, but his defenses were chemical rather than preferential; he tolerated rather than enjoyed alcohol—ordered a gin and tonic "with plenty of ice." Ice melted and became water, so his drink grew progressively weaker, which suited him fine.

The waiter came over with elegant oversized menus, and McCall saw Laurel study the righthand margins.

"Don't worry about the prices," he said. "I'm on a swindle sheet."

"I thought you were an honest man."

"I'm. But the governor gives me hell if I don't bill him with what he considers expenses appropriate to my position as his deputy. How about the steak-and-lobster combination?"

"Oh, my God," Laurel said. "I can't remember when I've had either. Yes!"

"It's been tough?" McCall said when the waiter moved away.

"Well." Laurel fiddled with her cocktail glass. "It hasn't been all roses and featherbeds. I come from a huge family, and every one had a mouth, every mouth was always hungry, and there was never enough of anything."

"How well I know," McCall said. "By the way, I noticed some books on the Peace Corps in your library. Were you once considering joining?"

"I did more than consider," Laurel said. "I joined."

"Really? You're the first girl I ever met who was in the Peace Corps. Tell me about it."

"I'm afraid it's not a very exciting tale," she laughed. "I wasn't one of those brave gals who lived in the Bolivian jungles and ministered to the "Indios" while fighting off the steaming advances of the Bolivian doctors. I spent two years in the Dominican Republic in a secretarial job."

"Where did you go to college?"

Her green eyes widened. "How did you know that?"

"I used to be a detective."

"No, I mean it! How did you know?"

"Those sociology and psychology books. They're college textbooks."

"I got a scholarship to State. I had to leave at the end of the first semester. My father died. I thought I wanted to go into social work."

The cocktail waitress brought Laurel's refill—McCall was still nursing his gin and tonic—and he dropped what was evidently a painful subject to her. "How did you happen to join the Peace Corps?"

"Why did men use to enlist in the Foreign Legion? I lost the boy I was engaged to. Vietnam."

"Oh. Rotten break."

"Oh, not to the V.C.," Laurel said brightly. "He married an army nurse. He's out of the service now. Settled in New York City, I understand, and raising a family like mad."

"He's an idiot."

"For raising a family like mad?"

"For leaving you for another girl."

"What a nice thing to say! And spoken as if you really mean it."

"I do."

"I'll bet. By the way, Lou's decision was a decision of honor. He got the gal pregnant."

"Well, Lou's loss is my gain," McCall said gallantly.

He asked her how she managed to snag the prestige job of secretary to the mayor. "I just applied for it when Mayor Potter's secretary quit to have a baby. The major events of my life," Laurel said thoughtfully, "seem

68

to result from other women's pregnancies. I wonder if there's a message there somewhere."

McCall chuckled and began to feel guilty. He had a premonition about this date, and it was making him so euphoric that the gravity of his mission for the governor seemed imperiled. He reached across the table for Laurel's hand, and she allowed him to hold it for a few moments before she firmly retrieved it. She began to ask him questions about himself.

"That's what the handbook says, all right," McCall said. "I mean the girl getting the man to talk about himself. How can I resist?" And he told her not quite all about himself. She was astounded to learn that he had been a private detective, first working for a national agency, then in his own business before quitting to become Governor Holland's man Friday.

"Mayor Potter said you were a lawyer."

"I passed my bar exams and found out that young law apprentices sit in cubbyholes preparing briefs or looking up stuff in bad-smelling law books. I can't stand desk work."

The cocktail girl asked if they wanted more of the same. Laurel shook her head. "Two is my limit. On three I get stupid, and on four I get sick. But don't let me stop you, Mike."

"I'm stopped," McCall told the waitress. "You can tell the waiter to serve dinner, miss, whenever he's ready."

During dinner McCall mentioned his unsuccessful attempts to reach Gerald Horton. "Do you think there's a chance of talking him into using his influence to get that bail reduced, Laurel?"

"I don't know him that well," Laurel said. "As councilman-at-large he's naturally in and out of the mayor's office, but he and Mayor Potter are hardly pals. I think they respect each other, but of course they're political opponents, and their relationship is correct rather than cordial. Mr. Horton extends it to me, too. He's never been more than polite."

McCall said gloomily, "Ben Cordes didn't hold out much hope of Horton's cooperating."

"The little man who runs Mr. Horton's radio station for him?"

"Yes. Horton's campaign manager."

Laurel paused in the process of dipping a forkful of lobster into her butter. "He is?" She seemed surprised.

"Not to mention writing Horton's speeches."

"So that's why he's at city hall so much! Some of us girls call him The Shadow because of the way he trots around after Mr. Horton. Will wonders never cease?"

She obviously knew nothing about the Horton setup— or considered what she knew confidential—so McCall turned to other subjects.

It was nearly eight-thirty when they reached the coffee. While Laurel was still sipping, McCall excused himself. The maître-d' directed him to a phone booth, and he tried Gerald Horton's number again.

This time he was successful. A deep, pleasant, phony voice said, "Horton residence."

"Mr. Gerald Horton?"

"Speaking."

"My name is Mike McCall, Mr. Horton—"

"Oh, yes, I've been expecting to hear from you, Mr. McCall. I just finished talking to Ben Cordes."

"Then you know why I'm calling."

"Ben and I discussed it at some length. I'm afraid my decision is what Ben told you it would be."

"There's a factor involved that I briefly mentioned but didn't discuss with Mr. Cordes in depth," McCall said. "It's my considered opinion, Mr. Horton, that this sky-high bail will provoke racial trouble in the city. You can't possibly want to risk that."

There was a silence. Then Horton said brusquely, "I don't agree, Mr. McCall. A demonstration, maybe. But Banbury doesn't have race riots."

McCall said just as brusquely, "I know, not since the 1920s. I read your Chamber of Commerce handout. Next year they may have to put out a revised edition."

"Mr. McCall. Are you sure there isn't a political motive behind this request of yours?"

It was McCall's turn to be silent. When he spoke it was tonelessly. "If you know anything about my relationship with Governor Holland, you know that my job is completely outside politics. The governor sent me down here for the sole purpose of heading off black-white violence, and I have made no secret of why I'm here. If politics is involved, it's your people who are playing it, Mr. Horton."

"What do you mean by that?" Horton sounded indulgent.

"I'll lay it on the line, Mr. Horton. I'm convinced that the charge against Harlan James and this one against LeRoy Rawlings are both calculated political maneuvers by District Attorney Volper. I think Volper wants to strain further the already tense race situation in this town in order to attract the votes of working-class whites to your law-and-order platform. I don't accuse you of being a party to this, Mr. Horton—"

"Thank you," Horton said dryly.

"—but on the other hand I'm not assuming your innocence, either."

"Who appointed you judge of my character, McCall?"

"I'm not judging you, sir. I'm here as an investigator, and any investigator worth his salt makes no unsupported assumptions."

"My whole career—"

"The political bug, Mr. Horton, invades the human economy in strange ways. However, that's not the point.

The point is that stirring up a racial stew here for political reasons was Volper's obvious motive in recommending this unconscionable bail to a handpicked judge. You may win the election by not lifting a finger to get that bail reduced, Mr. Horton, but you won't have as large a constituency to govern, because a lot of the voters will be dead."

Horton no longer sounded indulgent. "I regard this, McCall, as defamation of character!"

"So sue me," McCall suggested. "Meanwhile, let's stick to the immediate issue. Doesn't what I've said affect your attitude on the high bail in any way?"

"Not one damn bit!" Horton snapped, and he hung up with a crack.

When McCall returned to the table Laurel asked, "Any luck?"

"Oh, yes," McCall said. "All bad. I got hold of him, but he won't lift a finger. You think Mayor Potter or this lawyer Duncan he's backing to succeed him would have any influence with the judge?"

Laurel looked incredulous. "You must be kidding, Mike. Edmundson is a Horton man. Besides, he's a segregationist."

McCall shrugged. "Forget it, baby. While the city burns, let's fiddle."

So they spent the rest of the evening enjoying themselves. They watched the nine o'clock floor show, which was first-rate, and danced for a while. After the Capri they stopped into two other clubs. They had several more drinks apiece. Laurel became neither stupid nor sick. McCall allowed her only anemic gin-and-tonics.

He got her home after one in the morning. With what he hopefully interpreted as regret, she apologized for not inviting him in—she had to be up in six hours, she said, and she faced a big day.

"I'm one of those dreary people who need eight hours' sleep to function. I hope you don't mind, Mike."

"That's like asking the condemned man if the rope feels uncomfortable," McCall said. "Do I rate at least a good-night kiss?"

What happened then, brief as it was, made McCall curse his bad judgment all the way back to his hotel for not having got Laurel home earlier.

TEN

He was up by eight. He picked up a *Post-Telegram* to read with breakfast. The arrest of LeRoy Rawlings was not the lead story—a new Middle East eruption blasted it out of that position—but it was on the front page.

The story was headlined NO. 2 BLACK HEART CHARGED WITH CONSPIRACY. A subhead read *Bail Fixed at $50,000*. The story itself was an unsalted account of the facts.

McCall turned to the editorial page. The *Post-Telegram* vigorously disapproved of the excessive bail; it had nothing to say about the charge itself. Nor was there any comment about the possibility that the arrest might set off racial violence. Perhaps, McCall thought, it was just as well.

After breakfast he headed for Mayor Potter's office. The city hall opened for business at nine; it was about a quarter past when McCall turned into First Street.

Even from two blocks away he could make out the crowd packing the sidewalk and overflowing into the street before the city hall. As he approached he saw that the crowd was predominantly black. The sprinkling of whites seemed young and generally long-haired. He estimated the mob at 500. Perhaps one out of five was wearing a Black Hearts jacket.

The crowd was chanting, "Free LeRoy! Free LeRoy!"

The chant was ugly. McCall had observed such scenes frequently enough to read the temper of a mob from its tone. Any spark could set this one off.

The police had blocked off First Street before the city hall, apparently having abandoned an effort to keep it clear. A traffic officer was directing all vehicles to turn into Douglas Avenue, which was one-way at that point.

McCall maneuvered into the outer lane so that he could turn left halfway between First and Second into the municipal parking lot across from the big building.

By the time he had walked to the First Street exit from the lot, the mob had stopped chanting to watch what was going on at the top of the city hall steps. Mayor Potter stood there, rotund, white-thatched, flanked y a tall, very black man of thirty-five wearing glasses and a conservative brown suit, and a heavy, florid, fiftyish white man with graying hair. A workman in coveralls was setting up a microphone and a pair of speakers.

The silence of the crowd was more ominous than the chanting. McCall could only hope that the men on the steps would be convincing.

He decided to remain on the far side of the street instead of trying to force his way through the crowd.

The man in coveralls stepped aside. Mayor Potter immediately said into the microphone, "Can those in the rear hear me all right?"

The angry rejoinders of the crowd were hardly reassuring. The old man held up one hand.

"My friends of Banbury, I'm sure you all know these two gentlemen, but I will introduce them to any who may not. To my left is mayoralty candidate Mr. Jerome Duncan."

He turned in the direction of the black lawyer. There were a few cheers and some handclapping; hardly an ovation. McCall told himself that the reaction was not necessarily an index of lukewarm support by the black people of Banbury for Duncan's candidacy; it probably meant that the mob was in no mood for cheering anyone.

Mayor Potter nodded the other way. "To my right is Councilman-at-Large and opposing mayoralty candidate Mr. Gerald Horton."

75

A few boos; no applause. The crowd was too exercised over the Rawlings issue to be interested in political introductions.

"Mr. Duncan, Mr. Horton, and I have just held a conference," the old mayor went on. "We've agreed that it is essential to the welfare of this city that the three of us stand shoulder to shoulder on one issue, in spite of political differences. That area of agreement is this: that violence must not be allowed to shatter the peace of our city. We want you to know that we sympathize with your cause, and we pledge our combined legitimate influence to try to bring about what you demand. If you'll bear with us in patience, my friends, we three will confer with Judge Edmundson and request an immediate reduction of Mr. Rawlings's bail. We will do so the moment Judge Edmundson arrives in his chambers."

So the sight and sound of the mob had changed Gerald Horton's mind. McCall grinned to himself. That chanting had been considerably more convincing than a mere governor's emissary's voice over the telephone.

McCall was impressed by Heywood Potter's astuteness. The only man of the three standing before the crowd who was going to exert any influence on Judge Edmundson was Gerald Horton. But through the old man's ploy the incensed people would give as much credit to Potter and the man he had endorsed to succeed him, Duncan, as to Horton.

Someone shouted, "That's not enough, Mayor! We want all charges dropped against LeRoy! And Harlan, too!"

"Now, now, talk sense," the mayor replied. "You all know that any such promise from me wouldn't mean a thing. I'm the mayor, not a judge—I have no authority to suspend charges against anyone in a legal proceeding. I have no control over the district attorney, who is an employee of the county, not the city. And I certainly have no control over the district court, which is under the jurisdiction of the state. Nor can either of these gentlemen here with me exercise any more influence in these matters than I can. However, I do go on record, here and now, as being opposed to the prosecution of either Harlan James or LeRoy Rawlings."

There was far more applause this time, mingled with a few dissenting voices. A man in a Black Hearts jacket yelled, "Then why don't you get the D.A. and the judge out here?" Another roared, "We want action, not talk!" One deep voice overrode the others: "How do Duncan and Horton feel?"

The mayor glanced at the black candidate and stepped aside. The crowd fell silent as Jerome Duncan stepped over to the microphone.

"I feel the same way Mayor Potter does. I favor dropping all charges against Mr. James and Mr. Rawlings. Not because I'm a black man and they're black, too. I'd say the same thing if they were colored purple—or white. Those two men haven't done anything wrong. I'm against persecuting innocent people. As I'm sure every decent citizen of Banbury is."

The applause was prolonged.

"Mr. Horton?" the mayor said.

Horton was on the spot. McCall wondered how he was going to wriggle off. But the councilman-radio station owner calmly took the microphone and said, "I believe in law and order with justice. These men have been charged with certain offenses against the law, and I defend their constitutional right to a fair and speedy trial *according* to the law."

He was about to say more, but the boos swelled and drowned him out. A few whites were cheering, but they had no chance against the volume produced by the black throats. McCall saw Mayor Potter jerk Horton's coattails as Laurel Tate hurried out of the building to whisper in His Honor's ear.

The mayor stepped before the microphone and shouted, "Please! People, please!" It was surprising how his high-pitched old voice carried. Over the subsiding noise he shouted, "I'm informed that Judge Edmundson has just arrived. If you'll all stand by, we will confer with the judge and come right back here to report his decision to you!"

Potter herded Horton and Duncan before him like a fussy shepherd, Laurel bringing up the rear. The four of them disappeared in the recesses of the city hall.

The crowd buzz-buzzed, shifted feet; there was even some laughter. McCall felt a great relief.

He walked up to the corner, circled the crowd, and entered the city hall by one of the side doors. He found a directory that told him the municipal court was on the second floor.

He climbed dirty marble steps. The courtroom was empty, but a bailiff stood at the doors. When McCall glanced in the man said, "Court doesn't open till ten this morning."

"I was looking for the mayor."

"He's in chambers with Judge Edmundson, Mr. Horton, and Mr. Duncan. He can't be disturbed now."

McCall could have joined the conference as an observer, but he decided not to. His presence could add nothing; indeed, any suggestion of pressure from the governor's representative might upset the negotiations. He returned downstairs to the mayor's office to wait.

Laurel was alone. Her eyes were like green glass this morning—not enough sleep. McCall grinned. She was sipping coffee from a plastic cup.

"Hi."

"Hi," he said. "You're looking mighty pretty after all that dissipation last night."

"You're suffering from delusions, Mr. McC, or else you had nasty dreams last night. Coffee?" A small urn and a stack of plastic cups stood on a corner table.

"If it's good."

"It's very good. I brew it myself."

He drew a cup of coffee and went over to sit on the edge of Laurel's desk while he drank it. It was very good indeed, as advertised.

"You have many virtues, O Flame of the Occident," McCall said. "I may decide to make a play for you."

"Well, that's honest," Laurel said calmly. "Although honesty will get you nowhere. I mean not necessarily."

"You're also a tease."

"What woman isn't? I like my men to dangle."

This went on for some time. Two cups later McCall heard the mayor's amplified voice pierce the windows.

"Ladies and gentlemen! May I have your attention?"

They ran to the nearest window. The mayor, the councilman-at-large, and the lawyer were back on the steps.

"The court is dropping all bail requirements in the case of LeRoy Rawlings and releasing him on his own recognizance."

Wild cheering, clapping, whistling. The old man held up his hand and the crowd quieted again.

"The court clerk has already phoned the police officer in charge to have Mr. Rawlings in court here at ten o'clock—less than half an hour from now—so that he may be officially released."

More cheering.

McCall said to Laurel, "For an old warrior like Mayor Potter, that was bad tactics. Instead of breaking up, they'll hang around to see Rawlings and carry him off in triumph."

He was proved a prophet. The mayor piped, "I appeal

79

to you good people now to disperse. You've blocked traffic for some time now, so please all go home and let the business of the city hall area proceed normally."

No one stirred. The mood of the mob had changed from anger to festivity. The blacks, at least, were not going to be denied the sight of their hero.

Mayor Potter hesitated, his eye on the police officers at the barricades. But then he shook his head, smiled, waved to the crowd, and beckoned Duncan and Horton.

The man in the coveralls stolidly began to pack up the public address apparatus.

ELEVEN

A few moments later Potter, the councilman-at-large, and his lawyer-opponent entered the mayor's office. Jerome Duncan offered a warm black hand on being introduced to McCall, but Horton's handshake was perfunctory and he was wearing his political poker face.

"Mr. McCall and I had a telephone conversation last night," he said to the mayor.

"You seem to have come around to my point of view, Mr. Horton," McCall smiled.

"About that high bail sparking trouble, yes. Last night I thought you were exaggerating the danger. But you were right—that mob out there was really ready to bust out. I still resent your uncalled-for remarks about our district attorney, though."

McCall looked Horton in the eye. "I don't retract a damned thing I said about Volper, Mr. Horton. The provocatively high bail was set at his urging. Unless he's a complete fool, he had to have known what he was doing —lighting a match near an open gas tank. This town was ready to go up, Mr. Horton. It may still do it if Volper isn't restrained."

"What's going to blow," Jerome Duncan said, "is Volper. The D.A.'s office will have to be represented at the bail hearing, so the court clerk's undoubtedly phoned Volper's office."

"You people," Gerald Horton said coldly. "McCall here accuses Art Volper of deliberately inciting to riot for political reasons. Do you believe Art's capable of doing that, Duncan?"

The black man smiled without humor. "I wouldn't go

that far without *res gestae* evidence. But you have to admit, Horton, your boy Art isn't exactly objective where the Black Hearts are concerned."

"Neither am I," Horton snapped. "Any law-abiding citizen has a duty to oppose an outfit that preaches revolution."

"It hasn't been established that the Black Hearts preach revolution," Mayor Potter said gently. "Harlan James hasn't come to trial yet."

The councilman-at-large made an impatient gesture. "Did you listen to James's taped speech yesterday?"

McCall said, "I did. James won't ever take his place in the history books alongside Tom Paine, but his speech certainly didn't preach revolution."

"It preached violence! When a black man publicly urges other blacks to beat whites with baseball bats and blast them with shotguns, what can you call him except a violent revolutionary?"

"Wait a minute," Duncan said in a hardening tone. "He recommended those things only in retaliation against white attack. That's recommending self-defense."

"Oh, come on, Duncan! This guy has been preaching violence at his Black Hearts rallies ever since he formed the organization."

"How many Black Hearts rallies have you attended?"

"All right, none. But Ben Cordes went to a number of them when he was researching the special program we did on black militants last month. Cordes's reports of what was said at those meetings convinced me the organization is dangerous."

The phone on Laurel's desk rang. She answered it. "Mr. Cunningham for you, Mr. Mayor."

"I'll take it inside, Laurel," the mayor said. "You gentlemen want to come in?"

Both candidates said they had to run along. The

mayor waved and went into his private office. Jerome Duncan pressed McCall's hand in a friendly way.

"I'm afraid you haven't seen much of the better side of our town, Mr. McCall," he said. "There is one, you know. Mayor Potter's done a great job for the poor here, getting federal money for projects we desperately need—and you know what a magic trick that is these days. I hope, if I'm elected to succeed him, I can continue his good work."

"I have to stay politically neutral, Mr. Duncan," McCall said, straight-faced. "But I can say without hesitation that the governor is all for good works."

"So I understand," Duncan said, smiling. He had a million-dollar smile that made McCall think again of Carl Stokes. "That being the case, Mr. McCall, you might remind the governor that Banbury could use a lot more state money, too. See you." He nodded to Horton very politely and left.

"Well," Gerald Horton said. "I have to be going, too." He did not offer his hand. "Goodbye, Mr. McCall."

"Goodbye," McCall said. "Sorry we disagree about Volper, Mr. Horton. I wish you could see him the way I do."

"I couldn't disagree more," Horton said. He sounded very nasty. "Our district attorney is a conscientious public servant and patriotic American who's hitting hard at an outlaw group that needs hitting. I'm delivering a major political speech tonight, incidentally, and if you listen you'll hear me uphold Mr. Volper's actions in a most positive way."

"Benjamin Cordes mentioned something about a Horton rally tonight. Where is it being held, Mr. Horton?"

"At the Steelmen's Union Hall, on the south side."

"What time?"

"Eight."

83

"I'll do my best to catch it."

"Yes," Horton said icily. "Do that."

He turned on his heel and stalked out.

"I ought to turn up all the thermostats," Laurel said. "That voice of his is what I've always imagined the touch of a dead hand must be like. How about taking me to that rally, Mike?"

"Oh," McCall said swiftly. "I wish I could, Laurel, but I'm committed elsewhere. I wouldn't condemn you to a political speech, anyway—not one of Horton's."

He wondered why she gave him such an odd look. The truth was, he had almost forgotten his date for the evening with Chief Condon's blonde secretary, Beth McKenna.

"Serves me right for throwing myself at you," Laurel said lightly. "Now I really have to get back to work." And her typewriter began rattling away.

McCall went into Mayor Potter's office. The old man had just hung up.

"One of my staff," Potter said. "BOKO's announced over the air that another tape from Harlan James arrived in this morning's mail. They're going to broadcast it at ten."

McCall glanced at his watch. It was five of ten. "I'll have to miss it, Mr. Mayor. I want to be in court when Rawlings gets his bail hearing."

The marble staircase was clogged with people who wanted to get into the courtroom. Police were clearing the jam without difficulty; the mood of the crowd was docile, even good-humored.

McCall's shield case got him into the courtroom again. He estimated the spectators as ninety percent black; about half the men wore Black Hearts jackets.

Although it was now a few minutes past ten, the judge was not yet on the bench. The defendant was not in evidence, either. His lawyer, Wade, sat at the defense table, his face unreadable. But McCall thought he must be feeling good.

Arthur Volper was not present. A young assistant D.A. sat alone at the prosecutor's table. He seemed nervous.

A few moments later LeRoy Rawlings was brought in by Sergeant Fenner. The black-jacket wearers gave their vice president a standing ovation when he strode in. Grinning, Rawlings clasped hands above his head like a boxer acknowledging the acclaim of his fans.

Sergeant Fenner turned his prisoner over to a bailiff and left. He threw McCall a friendly wave as he went by.

Rawlings had no sooner seated himself beside his lawyer than the judge stalked in and everyone rose. Edmundson was a small, twitchy man in his fifties with thinning sand-colored hair, a case of acne, and a sour expression. He rapped with his gavel and said in an irritated voice, "Be-seated-court-is-now-in-session-will-the-attorneys-of-record-approach-the-bench."

The hearing took minutes. The assistant district attorney entered a learned objection to any reduction in the defendant's bail; the judge snipped him short.

"This is not an adversary proceeding. The matter is up to the discretion of the court, and my decision is made. Let's not waste any time, Mr. Browning!"

He then suspended bail, released the defendant on his own recognizance, and called the next case. As Rawlings started up the center aisle with his attorney, most of the spectators rose to follow. Judge Edmundson pounded with his gavel.

"Spectators will remain seated!" he shouted. "I will not have my courtroom disrupted by a mass exodus! You may leave at the first recess."

McCall was already out in the hall. As the courtroom door closed behind the two black men, he said, "Just a minute, Mr. Rawlings."

Both men turned. The Black Hearts vice president said in a neutral tone, "Hello, McCall."

"This is Mike McCall?" The lawyer held out his hand. "Roy told me how you gave Art Volper a lecture in constitutional law, Mr. McCall. Wish I'd been there to watch."

McCall shook it, smiling. "I think the D.A. knows his law, Mr. Wade. He just stretches the rules a little. Glad to meet you."

Rawlings stared at him. "Just what is Sam Holland's interest in the Black Hearts? If he didn't have an ax to grind, you wouldn't be smelling around."

"LeRoy," Wade said.

"It's not the Black Hearts alone that brought me here," McCall said. "It's the threat of race trouble. The governor wants me to head it off if I can."

"But it's very simple," Rawlings drawled. "Order Volper to drop the charges against Harlan and me, and tell Judge Graham to revoke Harlan's bail forfeiture."

McCall looked the black leader in the eye. "Oh, come on, Rawlings. You're not talking to an idiot, and I'm not talking to one, either. You know the governor has no authority to 'order' things like that. Are you and the Black Hearts bent on playing Volper's game? Apparently he'd like nothing better than a full-scale riot situation in this town. It would certainly polarize the white backlash sentiment. If it were bad enough, it would make headlines and newscast lead-offs nationally, giving Volper a showcase he couldn't get otherwise in a hundred years. You can't be that stupid."

"Don't call me stupid, man," Rawlings said. The whites of his eyes were shot with blood. "Don't ever! I'm not playing any game. It's the black brothers and the black community that take all the punishment when a ghetto burns. The lousy few honky merchants who lose a few

TV sets and some plate glass hardly count, considering the profits they've squeezed out of blacks for generations. When Whitey pushes too hard, man, nobody's going to stop blacks from pushing back! Avoiding showdowns is up to you honkies."

"LeRoy," the black lawyer said again; he was distressed.

"I don't want to get into a hassle about whose fault it will be if the city burns down," McCall said. "I just want to keep it from burning down. And if you'd seen that mixed mob in front of the city hall this morning, you'd realize how close this town was to being reduced to ashes. Do you think Harlan James would be willing to use his influence to cool tempers in case another incident like this morning's develops?"

"What influence does a fugitive in hiding have?" Rawlings asked bitterly.

"I'd like to discuss that with Mr. James personally. Can you arrange for me to see him?"

Rawlings's response was immediate and automatic. "Now how would I know where he is?"

"Mr. McCall," Prentiss Wade said. "Even if LeRoy knew, arranging for you to see Harlan would amount to an admission that the charge against him is true. At least that would be the district attorney's construction. Be reasonable."

"You have my word as Governor Holland's emissary that nobody but the governor will learn about it from me. In fact, I don't even have to know where Mr. James is. I'm perfectly willing to be blindfolded. All I want is a face-to-face talk."

"No, LeRoy, wait a minute," the black lawyer said. "What could your seeing Harlan James accomplish, Mr. McCall?"

"He keeps sending taped speeches to BOKO. Another

87

was scheduled for broadcast at ten this morning." He glanced at his watch. "It must be over by now. I'd hope to persuade him to make a public plea for restraint."

Rawlings showed his teeth. "I've already told you I don't know where he is."

"I find that hard to believe, Mr. Rawlings."

"I don't give a damn what you believe, honky, y' hear?"

McCall's eyes narrowed. "Up to now I considered this a conversation among reasonable men. Why the name-calling all of a sudden, Rawlings? You must know my reputation for fair dealing—"

"You don't cut it, huh? 'Honky' pulls you uptight, huh? Now you know how a brother feels when a honky calls him nigger!"

"I never in my life called anyone a racial or ethnic name," McCall said coldly. "And I'm damned if I'm going to let you put me on the defensive! I heard you were an intelligent man. I'm beginning to doubt the rumor."

The black face thrust close to his. "What kind of crap you dishing out, McCall? You never counted eenie, meenie, minie, moe when you were a kid? You always called those big nuts Brazil nuts? Huh?" His big fist gathered up McCall's jacket. "Answer me!"

"LeRoy, I want you to take your hand off Mr. McCall," the black lawyer said quietly. "Right now."

"It's all right, Mr. Wade," McCall said. "I could dump your client, big as he is, on his tokus without blinking an eye if I wanted to. Listen to me, Rawlings. Oh, first let go of my coat." Rawlings expelled some breath. Then his hand went slack. "Thank you. I grew up on Chicago's south side. The first kid I ever had a fist fight with was black. We gave each other bloody noses, and I don't know which of us was more surprised that we both had red blood. We became close friends. I'd never call you a

88

nigger, Rawlings. But I'm not so sure I wouldn't call you a jerk."

Rawlings grinned suddenly. "Okay, McCall, I withdraw honky. But I still can't help you. Yesterday I got a letter in the mail from Harlan, and it said about the same thing he wrote to the radio and TV stations. He said to tell the other Black Hearts not to worry about him, that he was okay, but he wasn't going to let any of us know where he was so the pigs wouldn't be pressuring one of us to tell."

Prentiss Wade frowned. "You didn't mention that to me, Roy. Where is this letter?"

"I tore it up."

"Tore it up?" Wade cried. "That letter could have helped your defense against this charge!"

Rawlings looked crestfallen. Then he shrugged. "Too late now, Prentiss. We get our mail in the morning, and I wasn't arrested till afternoon. How was I to know I was going to need a defense?"

McCall said, "Let me put it this way. If Harlan James does let you know where he is, will you ask him if he's willing to see me?"

"I'll think about it," Rawlings said. "Where do I reach you?"

"I'm staying at the Banbury Plaza."

Rawlings turned about. "Come on, Prentiss, I want to get home and wash the stink of that jail off me."

He walked away without a glance. Prentiss Wade smiled at McCall, spread his hands in humorous despair, and hurried after his client.

TWELVE

Officer Beth McKenna lived in a better residential district and apartment building than Laurel Tate's. Her apartment was in a twelve-unit, one-story building shaped like a squared-off C, legs pointing toward the street with a lawned courtyard between. There were outside doors to each apartment giving onto a parapeted porch that ran around the inside of the C.

Beth's was Apartment 3, on the left side of the porch. She came to the door in a white long-sleeved blouse with a mannish collar and a bowtie that matched her blue skirt. The ensemble managed to be anything but masculine. Her skirt was a miniskirt, the shoes were fashionable, and she had on sheer black butterfly stockings.

Having last seen her in her uniform, with a regulation-length skirt, McCall had not noticed her legs. He noticed them now—if "notice" was the word—the instant she opened her door. They were long and svelte, from a Vargas drawing. His inspection lingered.

"I have a face," Beth reminded him from her doorway.

"And a lovely one it is, too," McCall said absently. "I'm not a leg man especially. Oh, I like legs, all right, but I'm really a sort of all points man—I mean all curves—with no particular anatomical hangups. May I come in?"

"From the way you looked at them," Beth said, not moving, "I'm not sure I ought to let you."

"I'm perfectly harmless," McCall protested. "It's just that they were out here in the open to see, and if anything I'm farsighted. If they're not supposed to be looked at, why not try a maxi?"

She laughed. "At least you don't wallow in clichés. My

90

last date's original comment was, 'Boy, you got nice stems.' Come in."

The apartment seemed to be a three-roomer, like Laurel's, but the two rooms McCall could see were bigger than Laurel's and furnished with better taste. Banbury police must earn more than secretaries, which was improbable; more likely, Beth's police-lieutenant husband had left her a lot of insurance. The living room had a real fireplace. A breakfast counter separated the living-room area from a full kitchen; it was large enough to include a table and four chairs. A door opposite presumably led to the bedroom and bath.

"I wasn't quite finished dressing," Beth said. "Do you want a drink?"

"I can wait," McCall said.

"Be right with you."

She emerged from the bedroom wearing a long-sleeved jacket that matched her skirt. It took her a mere ten minutes.

"What kind of food grabs you?" McCall asked.

"I feel Italian tonight."

"Italian it is. Any recommendations?"

She hesitated. "Well, there's Luigi's over in the Italian section of town, but—"

"I'm on an expense account," McCall said. "Is it the best Banbury has to offer?"

"Positively."

"Then Luigi's is where we'll go."

They had excellent spaghetti, passable squid, and impossible Chianti. McCall praised it all as if it had been prepared by Mama Leone herself.

Over the espresso McCall asked her whom she favored in the mayoralty contest. "As a cop as well as a citizen," he said.

"Most of the force is behind Horton," Beth said. "I was, too. Because of his law-and-order pitch, of course.

91

But I've begun to have doubts . . . Chief Condon keeps saying we need a mayor with a no-nonsense attitude toward the black militants, but maybe a black man in city hall would quiet the racial unrest so there wouldn't be trouble at all."

"Ever hear Horton speak?" McCall asked.

She shook her head.

"Like to? He's holding a rally tonight."

Beth lowered her cup. "You're breaking something to me gently, aren't you? You've been meaning to attend the rally all along."

He grinned. "I really ought to hear what Horton has to say. Would you mind, Beth?"

"It's the story of my life," Beth McKenna sighed. "Other girls get taken to night clubs—me, on my dates I wind up listening to windbags." She pushed her chair back. "Don't be a horse's patoo, Mike. It's part of your job. I bet I'll just *love* him."

The Steelmen's Union Hall was at South Nevins and Kosciusko, in the heart of Little Poland. It was a two-story building whose insides had been scooped out like a gourd's, probably a converted Civil War armory or riding academy; it looked old enough. It was used mainly for social events and community meetings.

About 500 folding chairs had been set up; most were occupied. The principals were already onstage when McCall arrived with Beth McKenna, but the program had not begun.

Two of the half dozen chairs at the rear of the stage were occupied by Gerald Horton and Ben Cordes. Three other men and a woman, all beefy, overflowed the other four chairs—unmistakably of the genus party worker. Horton's crimson face positively glowed with love for his people as he looked about, waving and nodding. Technicians had set up broadcasting equipment and were making last-minute adjustments.

They found seats in one of the rear rows, and McCall surveyed Horton's audience. It was almost entirely a blue-collar crowd—factory workers with their wives and girlfriends. Not surprising. What was surprising was the scattering of black faces.

He remarked, "I didn't expect Horton to have any black backers."

"Why not?" Beth retorted. "Some of them are as upset by the Black Hearts as the whites are. The polls give Horton around ten percent of the black vote."

McCall doubted that a "law and order" candidate like Horton could command anything like that proportion of black support, but he said nothing.

Tiny Ben Cordes hopped out of his chair and sprang to the lectern. He fiddled with the microphone, smiling and nodding to people in the front rows. Finally he held up his hand and the chatter stopped.

"Ladies and gentlemen, I'm not going to make a long spiel introducing our speaker of the evening. You all know whom you came to hear tonight, and you all know his record of achievement and service to our beloved city. If there's a public servant in Banbury's history who's worked harder than this man to make this a safe and decent town for your wives and children to walk the streets, I never heard of him—and I go back a long way. So, ladies and gentlemen, without further ado I give you our great councilman-at-large for the last four years—and the next mayor of Banbury—the Honorable Gerry Horton!"

The candidate rose, and his audience almost beat him to his feet. There was a thunder of applause and stamping shoes in the vast echoing chamber. McCall rose with the others, pulling Beth up with him. She glanced at him curiously, but he was applauding. So she applauded, too, grasping the point. This was no time or place to be a conspicuous minority.

Cordes backed toward his seat, clapping his little hands as he did so, then holding one of them up, as Gerald Horton leaned against the lectern, in a signal to the crowd. What Cordes was doing, McCall was interested to note, was urging even louder applause. This was for the benefit of the camera and microphones, of course. The crowd obliged. Horton kept smiling, nodding, waving, turning this way and that for the television camera. The roar swelled . . . Incredibly, above it McCall heard what sounded like a cork expelled from a champagne bottle.

That's funny, he thought. How could I hear a cork over this bedlam?

Beth McKenna had her left hand over her mouth. She was staring at the rostrum. With her right hand she was yanking at McCall's·arm.

A small flower, like a dwarf red zinnia, had blossomed in the middle of Gerald Horton's forehead. The councilman, still with a half smile, was sliding out of view behind the lectern.

Shot, McCall thought.

Shot!

He spun around. A man dressed in black—black suit, black turtleneck shirt, black gloves (McCall could not see his shoes, but they must be black, too,-he found himself thinking)—was just lowering what looked like a .22-caliber Woodsman target pistol from where he had been steadying it over the crook of his left arm. The man was tense and lean and a black domino mask covered the upper part of his face. Below it, McCall saw black skin, broad nostrils, fleshy lips; above it, an Afro hairdo.

A middle-aged couple stood between McCall and the aisle. By the time he squeezed past them the black man had darted through the entrance door and slammed it behind him. A moment later McCall tore it open. No one

94

else in the audience had moved. It was ludicrous, like stop-action in a film, everyone in a deep freeze.

I must make an easy target silhouetted against the light, McCall thought. He shut the door behind him. Horton's assassin was sprinting across Kosciusko Street toward an alley. McCall raced after him. The man wheeled at the alley's entrance and swung up the long barrel.

McCall dropped flat. This time the shot sounded like a dropped board smacking a hard surface. A bullet swished over his head.

The masked man vanished in the alley. McCall rolled to his feet and was almost run down by a car. The driver spotted him at the last instant, swerved violently, and blasted in panic as the car went by. McCall lost a crucial few seconds.

It was a short block from Kosciusko to the next street. McCall got into the alley just in time to see his man dart out the other end. A moment later he heard an engine start, and a shriek of tires. By the time he emerged from the alley the getaway car was gone. He loped back to the meeting hall, inhaling in gulps.

The doors were open now and men were running into the street.

"Take it easy," McCall called. "He got away, he got away."

He went back inside. The people who had been seated at the rear of the stage now surrounded Gerald Horton. Someone had dragged him away from the lectern. He was lying on the floor, supine, his once red face a muddy gray-green. His eyes were open and staring into a bank of lights. Ben Cordes was on his knees laboring to resurrect him.

A handful of special officers were trying to keep the crowd away from the rostrum. A few women were crying. It was an oddly orderly scene.

95

Beth McKenna grabbed his arm as McCall hurried down the aisle.

"Mike. Did you—? Did he—?"

He shook his head, and she shut up.

A half bald man from the audience was shoving his way up the wooden steps leading to the stage, shouting, "One side, please. Please, one side! I'm a doctor. Please?"

McCall wriggled ahead of him and ran interference. A moment later they were on the platform.

"This man's a doctor. Get out of the way. Cordes! Would you mind?"

The little man got to his feet and lurched aside. He looked dazed. He sank into a chair and stared at the floor.

McCall took one look at the hole in Horton's forehead and turned Beth around. He did not wait to hear the doctor's verdict.

"Is he dead?" Beth gasped.

"Yes."

He got her back up the aisle to a door which looked as though it led into an office. The door was unlocked. McCall found a switch and turned on the light. He shut the door behind them and pointed to a phone on the desk. Beth looked at him, wide-eyed.

"You're a cop," he said. "Phone in."

THIRTEEN

Beth did not move. Instead, she shivered. "I'm really only a secretary, Mike. I don't know anything about things like this. You do it."

He remembered the number of police headquarters from having called Lieutenant Cox the day before. He dialed.

"You'll save time by asking for Communications," Beth said.

"Police Headquarters."

"Communications, please."

A moment later a female voice said, "Communications, Toomey speaking."

"This is Micah McCall, Assistant for Special Affairs to Governor Holland. I'm phoning from the Steelmen's Union Hall at South Nevins and Kosciusko."

"Yes, Mr. McCall?"

"Councilman-at-large Gerald Horton has just been shot and killed. Assassin was a black male, five eleven to six one, one seventy to one eighty, dressed in a black suit, black turtleneck Italian-style shirt, probably black shoes, no hat. Wears his hair Afro style. Age indeterminate—his face was half covered by a black mask. The only facial description I can give is that his skin is very dark and nose and lips characteristically Negroid. The weapon was a .22 caliber Woodsman target pistol. Got that?"

"Yes, sir." Communications' voice sounded shaky.

"Killer was last seen running south down an alley across the street from the union hall between South Nevins and whatever street lies east of it. He headed west—I think—on the street just south of Kosciusko, in an automobile. I only heard the car take off, I didn't see it, so I can't describe it. You'd better get all this right on the air."

"Yes, sir," the dispatcher said. "Were there any other witnesses?"

"Would you believe around five hundred?" McCall said.

"Thanks for phoning in, Mr. McCall. Please stand by there till the police arrive."

He hung up.

Beth said, "You know whom that description fits, don't you?"

"LeRoy Rawlings, Jerome Duncan, and maybe ten thousand other black men in town. Those bushy haircuts seem to be popular with all types and classes of blacks, regardless of political philosophy. The man's lips seemed a little thick for Duncan, but Rawlings has lips like that."

"So does Harlan James. Plus he's six one and weighs about a hundred and seventy-five pounds."

McCall looked interested. "You think maybe the troubles the Black Hearts founder's been having made him blow his cool?"

"He's human, isn't he? Did Communications give you any instructions?"

"Just to stand by until the law gets here. Excuse me while I make another phone call."

Maggie Kirkpatrick would probably not be at her newspaper this time of the evening. McCall looked up her home number.

"Mike McCall. Maggie?"

"Yes, indeedy, Mr. Big," Maggie's voice said. "What's on your mind that won't get you in trouble with the operator, if she's listening in?"

"Haha," McCall said. "I have another tip for you."

"Oh?" Maggie said.

"Do you want it?"

"Between the eyes. Shoot."

"Gerald Horton's just been shot and killed by a black man. Between the eyes, by a coincidence."

"Oh, no," she said. "No . . ." But then she said, "Tell me more, Mike!"

McCall told her.

"Thanks heaps! I owe you. Anything I can do for you?"

"Nothing at the moment, Maggie. This is just out of the goodness of my heart."

"I've heard about your heart," Maggie Kirkpatrick said thoughtfully. "Something tells me I'm going to pay for this. Thanks, Mike, and get off my line. I've got a story to phone in."

Something was happening in the hall. The hush did not seem healthy to McCall.

"Why the hell weren't some regular police assigned to the rally?" he growled. "I thought every city has an ordinance to that effect. What good are these specials? Look at 'em—scared to death. What's going on?"

Beth said nervously, "It's only been a few minutes since they got the word, Mike. What are you nervous about? It's so quiet."

"That's what I'm nervous about."

It had been a prelude to the trouble. Because now an argument swelled near the stage, men's voices, shaky with passion. McCall seized Beth's arm and headed her down-hall.

Except for Ben Cordes, the people onstage were still near the apron, but they were no longer clustered around the body. All of them, including the doctor, now crowded at the edge of the platform looking down at the disputing parties. Cordes was still seated on his folding chair, head in his hands.

The argument was between a powerful black man and

a burly white man with the veined and doughy face of a heavy drinker. McCall noted with disquiet that the black people of the audience had instinctively grouped themselves at the wall behind the black disputant, while several dozen white men had gathered behind his opponent.

The white man was saying hotly, "I ain't talking about people like you and these other black folks here tonight, Eddie. We know you're all all right. Jeeze, you guys are union brothers. But you saw what we saw—it was a black shot him."

"So what?" the man called Eddie cried. "What's the color of his skin got to do with anything? Don't you lump me with that killer—whoever he is!"

"He's a Black Heart, Eddie—"

"How do you know what he is? I never saw him before in my life, and neither did you!"

"Ah, what are you arguing with this guy for?" one of the white men yelled. "You're wasting your breath, Joe—"

"You're the kind starts riots," the black man yelled back. "I'm surprised you didn't come here tonight in sheets!"

"Now listen here, Eddie—" the white disputant began menacingly.

"The hell with him, Joe," his supporter shouted. "How about we go show them Black Hearts they ain't getting away with murder in our town?"

A deep foreign voice boomed, "The niggers want war, boys. I say we go get guns and wipe out Blacktown!"

The speaker was a lanky blond with chalky cheeks and ferocious gray eyes. The black man, Eddie, stepped up to him. "You want war, Zablonski, you got it right now." He cocked an enormous fist.

"Wait a minute, Eddie," the man named Joe said; he had apparently been having second thoughts. "Zablonski ain't calling you a nigger. He means the ones killed Horton."

"You don't even know who 'they' are! All I saw was one man. You're as bad as the Klan, you people. Your idea of justice is to run riot in the black ghetto and string up the first black man you see! Well, we're not going to let it happen! We—"

"*Shut up!*"

The sharp authority of the voice from the stage stopped everything dead.

"Listen to me, all of you!"

It was, unbelievably, Benjamin Cordes. He now stood glaring down from the edge of the stage. His face was pale with rage and his blazing eyes swept over the crowd with contempt.

"You listen to me!" he cried. "Gerry Horton, our leader, lies here dead, and all you can think to do is squabble about who's to blame. For your information Gerry headed off one race riot today, and I'll be damned if I'm going to let his death set off another. I helped him with tonight's speech, so I know what he was going to say. Part of his talk was going to be a plea for racial understanding. He believed in law and order, but he believed in brotherly love, too!" His voice rose. "Nobody's going to get guns and head for the west side ghetto. So shut your face, Zablonski, and you, too, Rozak!"

The two men addressed by name gawked up at him. Cordes turned to the big black man. "Eddie, I wouldn't blame you for walking out on the party after this. But try to understand that these men don't really mean it. They're just terribly upset by what's happened. Let's all cool off and be friends again. With poor old Gerry gone there's lots of thinking and planning to do, and it's going to take all of us thinking and planning together to pick up the pieces."

101

Something like a tremor went through the crowd, and then it was silent. In the silence the man with the alcohol-ravaged face threw the black man a sheepish smile and lightly punched his shoulder. The lanky Pole came over and said something. Eddie managed a smile.

"I guess Ben's right," he said, and the three men shook hands. The tension slacked at once. A low, friendly conversation broke out all over the hall, serious, sober.

McCall breathed. "I wouldn't have believed it. That little guy just nipped a roundhouse brawl in the bud. Not to mention saving whatever black votes the party would have lost."

"Cordes worshiped Horton," Beth said. "You just saw a kitten turn into a tiger."

McCall was looking around. "With five hundred other witnesses here, there's no point in us hanging around."

"But Communications told you to wait for the police."

"I didn't say I would. I've already told everything I know over the phone."

"But where do you want to go?"

"To a private phone. I've got to report this to the governor."

"You can use mine," Beth said. "I'd just as soon spend the rest of the evening at home, anyway, Mike. This didn't exactly put me in the mood for fun."

As they left the building they heard sirens. A city ambulance was racing up. Two police cars shot into view from opposite directions.

McCall helped Beth into the rented car, shaking his head.

McCall was still waiting for his call to get through when Beth emerged from her bedroom. She had got rid of her jacket and handbag, kicked off her shoes, removed her bowtie, and unbuttoned the top button of her blouse.

102

"I turn slob as soon as I get home," she said, sailing by him into the kitchen. "Gin and tonic?"

"Short on the gin. It may be a long night."

"I'll get you comfortable, too, after I mix the drinks."

Her remark did not register. The operator chose that moment to locate Sam Holland at the gubernatorial mansion.

"Something wrong, Mike?"

"A disaster, Governor. A half hour ago Gerald Horton was gunned down by a masked black man at a political rally. He was dead before he hit the floor."

As he recounted what had happened, Beth tugged at his coat collar. He leaned forward on the stool—her phone stood on the breakfast bar—and let her pull his right sleeve off, then his left, hardly aware of what she was doing. She took his coat into the kitchen and hung it over a chair.

When McCall finished, Governor Holland was silent. Then he said, "That black-white confrontation in the hall you just described, Mike, sounds like an omen of things to come. If the assassination arouses a strong rightwing reaction, you may face the inverse of what I sent you down there to stop—whites rioting against blacks instead of the other way around. And if a white backlash should gain any substantial support, it will take more than that radio station manager to head it off."

Beth was removing McCall's necktie. She unbuttoned his top shirt button, knelt, and began unlacing his shoes.

McCall took a sip of his drink, wiggling the toes of his first freed foot. "Even if no racial clash develops, Governor, this may kill the party's chances in the Banbury elections. With voting more than a full month off, they still have time to pick a substitute candidate. And with the boost the law-and-order issue got tonight, they might win with almost anybody."

103

Beth pulled off his other shoe.

"Do you have any idea whom they'll pick?"

"No. But Cordes ought to know. I'll drop by BOKO tomorrow and try to find out what we're up against."

"Okay, Mike. Keep me posted." The governor sounded funereal as he hung up.

Beth was just getting up from her knees. McCall drew her to him.

"You took advantage of a helpless man. How would you like it if I started taking off your clothes?"

"I might holler rape," Beth said. She made no attempt to get away. Her blue-violet eyes were soft.

"With that build? What jury would believe you? No man could rape you unless he knocked you unconscious first."

"So knock," Beth said. "I'll try to yell before the blow lands."

"Would you?"

"It's obvious you're no gambler."

"What do you mean?"

"Why don't you come up and try me some time?"

He spent the night there.

FOURTEEN

The masked black man was jabbing his shoulder with the muzzle of the target pistol, and every jab jarred him to his teeth. McCall opened his eyes to find Beth standing over him, poking him. She was dressed in her policewoman's uniform.

A tripartite aroma of frying bacon, toasting bread, and brewing coffee assailed his nose like an aphrodisiac.

"My God," McCall said. "I'm absolutely starved."

"Zoo fooding in ten minutes," Beth said. "I set you out a reserve toothbrush, but I've got nothing for you to shave with unless you want to try the electric I use on my legs."

"No, thanks! I'll leave the whiskers till I get back to my hotel. How about a good-morning smooch, or does the uniform make you off-limits?"

She stooped and gave him a motherly kiss on the forehead.

"Up, lover," she said, lithely dodging his reaching arms. "Not now. I've less than an hour to be at work, and it's a twenty-minute drive."

They parted at her front door.

"Will I see you again, Mike?" Her extraordinary eyes were sober and direct.

"After last night, isn't that a kind of silly question?" McCall murmured.

"Not really. Some men specialize in hit-and-runs. How do I know you're not one of them?"

"Even if I were, with you I'd be back for more."

"Oh?" Beth said. "And why is that?"

"When I was a kid in Chicago, there was a mean bastard of a cop who used to rap the kids across the seat of their pants with his nightstick to hear them squeal. I've been waiting my opportunity to make a cop squeal ever since."

Her tanned face flamed. "If you're referring to what happened last night—"

"Baby," McCall crooned, "you've got the nicest squeal I ever did hear."

"Also, you're no gentleman! Look, Mike, I have to run . . . call me—or something?" And she was gone.

McCall followed Beth's car downtown as far as the city hall, where she turned toward police headquarters. They exchanged goodbye honks, and he continued along First Street and turned right to the Banbury Plaza.

It was two minutes to nine when he stepped out of the shower. He switched the radio on and turned to BOKO to catch the news while he shaved.

The local news summary was almost entirely concerned with Gerald Horton's murder. Several black suspects had been questioned by police, the newscaster said, but all had been released; the police, who were not talking, apparently had no clue to the identity of the assassin. The newscaster did not identify the suspects questioned, but McCall had no doubt that one of them was LeRoy Rawlings.

He stopped in midstroke when the announcer moved on to Horton's party's problem of selecting a new candidate for mayor. The newscaster said:

"Banbury party chairman T. Ellsworth Yates has informed station BOKO that an emergency meeting of his executive committee was held secretly at his home last night. The committee unanimously selected BOKO station manager Benjamin Cordes as the late Gerald Horton's replacement as candidate for mayor, and Mr. Cordes was persuaded to accept the nomination, Mr. Yates said, only after long argument by the committee.

"With the election five weeks away, there is still time to meet the legal requirement to file intention to run for office thirty days in advance of election, Mr. Yates pointed out, so Mr. Cordes's name will positively be on the ballot. The chairman explained that if the election were being held just one week earlier, he would have had to rely on a write-in campaign. Mr. Yates expressed confidence that the new candidate will get the votes of all Gerald Horton's supporters.

"In his official announcement, Mr. Yates stated that Benjamin Cordes had been selected by the executive committee as the most suitable replacement for Mr. Horton for a number of reasons. As Horton's campaign manager the new candidate not only is thoroughly familiar with the campaign issues, but he played a major role in writing the party platform. Although not as well known by the general public, according to party chairman Yates, he is widely known and respected by party workers. Mr. Cordes has been particularly active, Mr. Yates said, in forming political clubs of factory employees; he has a wide acquaintanceship among the so-called blue-collar workers.

"The issues of the campaign will remain the same despite the change in candidacy, the party chairman announced. The main issue will continue to be the party's position that Mayor Heywood Potter's administration has been too permissive with militant minority groups and has hampered the city's police and prosecutors in upholding and enforcing the law."

So Ben Cordes has had the mantle of party leadership thrust on his chicken shoulders, McCall thought as he resumed shaving. He could imagine how much pressure the executive committee had had to bring to bear on the little man to "persuade" him to accept the nomination. By his own admission Cordes was a behind-the-scenes type who preferred working in the dark rather than in

107

the glare of open political warfare. But McCall had an idea that, once committed, Cordes would surprise a great many people. The little guy had potential.

The phone rang as McCall finished dressing.

"How come you didn't wait for us to get to the hall last night?" Lieutenant Cox asked in his melancholy voice.

"I had urgent business elsewhere," McCall said. "Besides you had five hundred other witnesses. Do you have a case?"

"Bloomfield and Speziale of Homicide took the original squeal. Fenner and I have the followup. The other five hundred didn't phone in, Mr. McCall, and you did. I've got to ask you to drop by here this morning."

"All right. Say fifteen minutes?"

He had planned to visit BOKO and Ben Cordes first, because the radio station was nearer the hotel than any of his other ports of call. But the summons from the lieutenant sounded a note of caution. Better not to cross the locals.

He drove over to police headquarters.

He found Lieutenant Cox and Sergeant Fenner in the detective bureau squadroom. The lieutenant wanted a signed statement.

"It's because you were the one who called in," Cox said apologetically. "You know the rules, Mr. McCall."

"I can't add anything to what I told Communications over the phone, but I'll be glad to repeat it for your file. Bring on your stenographer."

"Who rates stenographers?" Cox grunted. "Just tell it to Hank here. But take it easy, Mr. McCall. He not only doesn't know shorthand, he can hardly write."

"If I had to take off my shoes to count past ten, like you do, I wouldn't mention the next guy's educational shortcomings," Sergeant Fenner growled back.

It took McCall only a few minutes to tell his story,

which the sergeant took down in a cryptic shorthand apparently of his own invention. "I can hardly write, huh?" he said. "Okay, Lieutenant, you can read. Try reading this!"

"They didn't teach us hieroglyphics in the school I went to," the lieutenant said with dignity.

Fenner typed his notes and McCall signed the sheet.

"Anything else, Lieutenant?"

"Could you identify the killer if you saw him again in the same kind of half mask, Mr. McCall?"

"I don't know. I kind of doubt it. The nostrils, hair, lips, and skin color were typically African—characteristic of a great many black men. I might be able to cross off a few suspects for you, but I'd hesitate to make a positive I.D. on the basis of the mere glimpse I got of only half his face, even if it was the lower half." At the detectives' puzzled look McCall said, "I mean, the lower half of a face is better for identification purposes than the upper half. The really smart boys hide the lower part if they're going to use only a partial. This one either wasn't smart or he was lucky. Anyway, I don't believe I could identify him beyond a doubt. By the way, according to a radio report I heard, you fellows pulled in some people for questioning. Anyone I know?"

"One of them," Lieutenant Cox said. "LeRoy Rawlings. As usual he had an alibi for the time of the assassination. He was presiding over a meeting of the Black Hearts executive board, according to the sworn statements of five board members." The detective shrugged. "The Black Hearts always come up with alibis like that."

"Whom else did you question?"

"A few hatchet men who wouldn't be above making this kind of a hit for enough scratch. They had alibis, too. We were only seening, anyway, if we happened to catch them in the net. We had no particular reason to suspect them. Personally, I think the killer was Harlan James."

"Why?" McCall asked quickly.

"The description fits, he hated Gerald Horton's guts, and in my book he's off his rocker. Plus that gun."

"What about the gun?"

"Hank caught that," the lieutenant said. "Tell him."

Sergeant Fenner said, "I had a recollection that Harlan James applied for a permit to carry a hand gun a couple of years back. Though I had a feeling his application had been turned down; I checked with the files and, sure enough, he had applied and had been turned down."

"So?"

"On an application for a gun permit, you have to enter a description of the weapon you want to carry. What James applied for was a .22 caliber Woodsman target pistol."

FIFTEEN

He drove directly to BOKO.

The studio maintenance engineer, Andy Whalen, was coming down the hall when McCall stopped before Cordes's office door.

"Oh, Mr. McCall," Whalen said. He shook his big red head. "You hear what happened last night?"

"I was there," McCall said.

"Wasn't that something? They ought to line all those Black Hearts up against a wall and shoot 'em like dogs!"

"I happen to be a dog man myself," McCall said. "What makes you think the Black Hearts had anything to do with Horton's killing?"

"Who else could it be? You know what I think? It was that kook Harlan James himself. Don't you?"

"I could have been any one of thousands of people."

The ex-boxer looked uncertain. Then his battered features lit up. "Hey, what do you think about our boy Ben Cordes being tagged to run in Mr. Horton's place?"

"I don't know enough about Banbury party politics to say."

"Yeah, but can you imagine that little guy as mayor?" He laughed. "Not that he ain't smart enough, if you know what I mean—"

"I know what you mean. Well, Whalen, I'm in something of a hurry—"

"Yeah, I got to get going, too, Mr. McCall. Emergency generator's on the fritz. If the city power went out, we'd be off the air. See you."

McCall nodded.

The man went down the stairs. McCall rapped on the door of Cordes's office, opened it, glanced in.

111

"You busy, Mr. Cordes?"

"Mr. McCall. Come in. Have a chair."

McCall sat down. "Congratulations on your selection as candidate for mayor."

"Thank you," the little man said with a grimace. "I was the most surprised man there. I accepted only because I knew Gerry would have wanted me to. I was closer to him, I guess, than anybody else."

"You don't sound like a very enthusiastic candidate," McCall remarked. "Duncan doesn't strike me as a pushover."

"Oh, he isn't. But don't misjudge me, Mr. McCall." Cordes's tone hardened. "I was reluctant to accept the nomination because I hate public exposure and what hard-fought campaigns call on a candidate to go through. But now that I'm in it, I'm out to win. And make no mistake about that. I don't expect this pronouncement to bowl you over, Mr. McCall," Cordes went on with a faint smile, "inasmuch as the governor's backing Duncan, and maybe you think the little man is whistling in the dark to keep his courage up. If so, you can tell Sam Holland he and his party are making a big, a very big, mistake. As you'll all find out."

McCall smiled back. "My report to the governor is not going to underestimate you, Mr. Cordes. Anyway, don't include me in your collective 'you.' My personal politics aren't involved."

The little man squinted at him across his desk. "Why are you here this morning, Mr. McCall?"

"I wanted to talk about last night, and any developments subsequently."

"Yes, I understand you were present in the hall when the shooting took place. In fact, that you were the man who chased the killer and gave the police his description."

"That's correct."

"That was very courageous of you, Mr. McCall. Did you have a weapon?"

"Never carry one," McCall said. "And it wasn't courage, it was reflex. I used to be a Marine. However, thank you. I admire the way you stopped the trouble that was brewing there last night, by the way."

"We can all apparently call on reserves we didn't know we had," Ben Cordes said simply. "By the way, no one's mentioned it publicly yet as far as I know, but that description you gave the police fits Harlan James."

"And LeRoy Rawlings, and Jerome Duncan."

"Duncan!" The little man leaned forward. "You can't be serious, Mr. McCall!"

"I'm merely pointing out a possibility. I'm not accusing Duncan. He'd have to be a maniac to have done what that masked man did last night, and Jerome Duncan strikes me as anything but crackers. The point is, James is not the only black man in Banbury who fits the description."

"Oh . . . incidentally, we received another taped speech from James in the mail this morning, along with another letter. See what you make of this."

He handed over a sheet of cheap white bond paper. It was neatly typed, addressed to the radio station. There was no return address. The letter was dated the previous day:

Sir:

I heard on the news that Gerald Horton was shot to death earlier this evening by a black man. According to the broadcast description, that black man could have been me. It wasn't, but I suppose I'll be blamed for it.

I won't shed my black tears over the death of a racist honky, because Gerald Horton was an enemy

113

of my people. But I didn't kill him and I don't know who did. Not that Whitey will believe me. You racist pigs are out to get me one way or another, and if you don't frame me for this you'll frame me for something else. If you can find me, that is.

Enclosed is another taped message to my brothers. Since BOKO is the only station which has broadcast the first two, this is an exclusive—only you are getting this tape. In the future, as long as you continue to broadcast my tapes, BOKO will continue to receive them exclusively.

I won't thank you for playing them, because you wouldn't be doing it unless you thought it was gaining you listeners and profits. Your dead owner was a racist pig, so I imagine your news department is run by racist pigs also.

> *From the bottom of my black heart,*
> HARLAN JAMES

The signature was in ink over the typed name.

McCall handed the letter back. "He's a literate man."

"Articulate, too," Cordes said. "And no dummy, Mr. McCall. James just happens to be a fanatic. Does it sound to you as though he's intimating that he did kill Gerry, but phrased it in such a way that it doesn't constitute a confession?"

"No. I think he genuinely means this letter as a denial of guilt. I can see that some listeners might interpret it as a brag, especially if the thought is suggested to them. Do you plan to do that, Mr. Cordes?"

"We don't suggest anything to our listeners, Mr. McCall," the station manager-candidate said stiffly. "Our eleven o'clock newscaster—eleven A.M., that is—will read James's letter and play his tape. We played yesterday's tape at ten, but today our mail was late, so we couldn't squeeze it into the ten A.M. newscast unless we

114

ran it without screening it first. And we couldn't do that, because the usual obscenities have had to be blipped out."

"I'll try to catch it. I missed yesterday's."

"You didn't miss a thing," Cordes said in a grim voice. "Same old stuff about slavemasters and black-hating honkies and racist pigs."

"Why are you playing these tapes? They can only be incendiary."

"I'm running a radio station, Mr. McCall, and the tapes are news—exclusives, besides." Cordes shrugged. "I don't deny it worries me. But I'm a politician, Mr. McCall, not a social worker. For a smart man Harlan James in some ways is pretty dumb. It's this honky hangup of his—it blinds him to his own best interests and the interests of Banbury's black people generally. These speeches of his are alienating the white middle and blue-collar classes from Jerome Duncan's candidacy simply because they're delivered by a radical black; Duncan being black, too, he naturally gets tarred with the same brush."

"There's nothing natural about it," McCall said abruptly. "It's out-and-out prejudice."

"Isn't that natural?" Cordes asked with a slight smile. Then he shrugged again. "Anyway, that 'prejudiced' white vote is going to swing this election."

"But a quarter of your population is black. That's a healthy chunk of the electorate."

The little man shook his head. "We have some ten percent of the black vote tied up, and the power of the other ninety percent is overrated. Less than half the eligible black voters turn out on Election Day in this town, as opposed to about seventy percent of the whites. If the killer is caught before the election and turns out to be some Black Heart—especially if it turns out to be James —we'll walk in."

"And if it turns out that the Black Hearts had nothing to do with Horton's murder? All this propaganda pressure against them might well swing public opinion around and give Jerome Duncan the election by a sympathy vote."

Cordes smiled again, not slightly this time. "I read somewhere once that Bismarck said politics isn't an exact science. That's what makes it so fascinating. Anyway, the odds are against the case being solved by Election Day. The police don't seem to have a single clue."

"But they do," McCall said.

"Oh?" Cordes's nose twitched like Peter Rabbit's. "What's that?"

"I don't know that they want it publicized, so this is off the record. It concerns the weapon used. I'll be working on the case with the police, by the way."

The little man said, "I thought your mission here is to try to prevent a racial outbreak."

"It is. But cracking this murder may do exactly that. At the moment I'm more concerned with heading off white violence than quieting the blacks. Horton's being shot by a black will probably put a damper on black protest for the time being, but it's bound to whip up a white backlash. It could well have developed last night until you stepped in."

Cordes waved away the implied compliment. "Of course white violence can't but harm my candidacy, while black violence can't but help it. I don't like the choices. You can expect my full cooperation, Mr. McCall, any time you think you can use it."

McCall shook his head. "I have the feeling I'm going to need all the help I can get before this thing is settled. I want to see this murder cleaned up as quickly as possible—before the election, certainly. It seems to me our number one priority of business. And it has nothing to do with whether it's going to make it easier or harder for you to win, Mr. Cordes. I'm after peace in Banbury, as the governor directed."

"Amen." The little man shook his head. "And good luck. I know something about your reputation as a scalp hunter."

McCall rose. "Thanks for your time, Mr. Cordes. And for your offer. I'll call on you if I need your help."

It was pushing eleven when McCall headed for city hall. He turned his car radio on to BOKO.

In spite of Cordes's assurances, when the newscaster, a naturally nasal type, read the latest letter from Harlan James he employed an insinuating sneer that managed to give it a far different tone from the one McCall had got out of it. The letter, delivered in that tone, sounded so arrogant and braggart that McCall was convinced a large part of the listening audience would interpret it as a taunting challenge—a veiled admission that James had killed Horton.

Either Cordes had cynically lied to him, or the station's news department was overzealous. In any event, the damage was done.

Harlan James's taped speech was broadcast immediately after the reading of his letter. It was still going on when McCall got to the city hall. He pulled into the municipal parking lot and sat in his car listening to the rest of it.

It went on for fifteen minutes, a screed of violent invective and blipped-out obscenities against whites for oppressing blacks, a harangue that could only inflame both races.

Ben Cordes was right about the effect these speeches would have on white lower and middle-class minds. They were bound to arouse fear and hatred and turn too many people against the Black Hearts, and consequently against candidate Jerome Duncan for the sole reason that he shared the Black Hearts' blackness.

117

SIXTEEN

Laurel was alone in the mayor's reception room when McCall walked in. She was typing a letter. She glanced up just long enough to give him a brief cool look, then bent to her typing again.

McCall stood over her curiously. When she continued to ignore him, he said, "What's the matter?"

She went on typing. "The matter? Why should you think anything's the matter?"

"Don't you recognize me?"

Laurel typed away.

"I'm McCall, remember?"

He might not have been there.

"Baby girl." He snapped his middle finger off the ball of his thumb and blipped her in the middle of her nape. She jumped a foot and looked up wrathfully.

"You made me make a typo!"

"What's with the deep-freeze?" McCall demanded. "What have I done?"

Laurel began to doctor her error. She concentrated on the erasure. "Chief Condon just left the mayor. He stopped by to give the mayor a detailed report about last night. I had to sit in to take notes."

"So?"

"The chief said you were the one who first reported the murder."

"That's right. What of it?"

"He also mentioned that you attended the rally with his secretary, a Policewoman Mackenzie or something." She paused. "A female cop."

118

"McKenna, Beth McKenna. Very nice gal." Chief Condon had a big mouth, McCall decided.

"Oh?" Laurel laid down the fiberglass eraser, picked up one of rubber, and used it to erase the error on the second sheet. "How nice?"

"Very nice, I said," he said. "Were you a Horton backer?"

That startled her. "Of course not!"

"Policewoman McKenna was. Or at least she was thinking of becoming one. Her boss was backing Horton, along with most of the other members of the force, so she could attend the rally without repercussions. Could you have?"

Laurel considered this. "I suppose it would have looked funny. I mean with the mayor supporting his opponent."

"Exactly," McCall said. "Can you imagine the headline if some reporter had spotted you there? *Mayor's Secretary Backs Boss's Political Foe.* God, your hair. You never got that auburn out of a bottle! Busy tonight?"

"I'm invited to a baby shower." She continued to examine him. "I'll probably be home by nine."

"I'll be there at five past."

She laughed suddenly. "I think I'm being conned. But don't take my girlish laughter as weakness, Mr. McCall. I may decide to get mad all over again."

"Is it a date?"

"It's a date. Did you want to see the mayor?"

"That's one of the reasons I'm here."

"I assume that means I'm the other, but I'm not going to press my luck. Mr. Duncan's with the mayor." She jabbed at the intercom. "Mr. McCall is here, Mr. Mayor. Shall I have him wait?"

Mayor Potter's high voice said, "No, no, Laurel, send him in. I've been wanting to talk to him."

Jerome Duncan rose when McCall entered the office and offered his hand.

"You're looking at me hard, Mr. McCall," the mayoralty candidate said. There was a suggestion of amusement in his liquid eyes. "Do I fit the description?"

McCall grinned. "Touché. Put it down to occupational habit, Mr. Duncan."

"Black is black, eh?"

"No, sir. Just another point of identification, like blue eyes." The chitchat was on a light level, but McCall nevertheless took in the lower part of Duncan's face in detail. The skin was as dark as the killer's, but Duncan's lips and nose were too Caucasoid to match, he decided.

"How do I come out on your computer, Mr. McCall?"

"Aces high, Mr. Duncan."

"In that case, take one of the mayor's chairs." The candidate grinned at the old man. "Sorry to monopolize the conversation, Heywood, but I had to find out where I stood with the governor's man."

"Why don't we all sit down?" Mayor Potter said. He settled himself in his highbacked black swivel chair. "Chief Condon just left here, Mike. Dropped in to brief me about last night."

"Your secretary just told me."

"I don't know what's happened to this country," the old man said, shaking his head. "The Kennedys, Dr. King, now Horton—terrible. Any ideas on the Horton killing you didn't express to the police, Mike?"

McCall hiked his eyebrows. "No. Why do you ask?"

"My police chief is convinced the killer was either Harlan James or some other Black Heart acting under James's orders." The mayor gestured toward a radio on a bookcase. "BOKO got another letter and tape from James in this morning's mail, and we heard the broadcast while Chief Condon was here."

"I caught it on my car radio."

"It didn't do anything to change the chief's mind about James's guilt," the mayor said. "Condon's so locked in on it, I'm afraid he won't look elsewhere for an answer."

"The question is why he's so locked in on it, Heywood," the black candidate said. "The man's a racist, you know that. You should have replaced him long ago."

"You know that would turn the police department upside down and inside out, Jerome. As strong as the department feeling is, they're still a functioning force, and I can't afford to leave my city without effective policing."

"I wonder," Duncan said. "Ask our black citizens how effective they consider the Banbury police. Their definition, Heywood, might be different from yours."

"No sense in arguing," the mayor said. "I'm mayor of the whites as well as the blacks, and I have to do what I consider best for everybody. When you're mayor, you'll find out what I'm talking about. Right now, Condon's worrying me."

"Don't let him, Mr. Mayor," McCall said. "The two men assigned to the case are good cops. They lean toward James as the prime suspect, yes, but that won't keep them from investigating other possibilities. And even if they shouldn't, I'll be probing on my own."

Jerome Duncan leaned forward. "You're going to assist in the investigation, Mr. McCall?"

"More than assist. I like to work in cooperation with the local authorities, but only so far and so long as they're doing a job. Cooperation has never kept me from striking out on my own."

Duncan studied him. "Who are the men in charge of the case?"

"Lieutenant Cox and Sergeant Fenner of the detective bureau."

The black man nodded. "They're a good team. Do they have anything to work on?"

"One clue that points to Harlan James."

"What's that?"

"I don't imagine they want it broadcast," McCall said. "While it points to James, it doesn't convict him by a long shot."

McCall stopped in the outer office to use Laurel's phone book.

Harlan James was not listed. McCall looked up James's sister, Mrs. Franks. A number of Frankses were listed, but none had the Christian name Isobel or the initial *I*.

He called the *Post-Telegram* city room and caught Maggie Kirkpatrick at her desk. Yes, Maggie said, she knew Isobel Franks's address; she had been to Mrs. Franks's home several times on assignments to interview the president of the Black Hearts.

"She never changed the phone listing after her husband Cecil died a few years back," Maggie said. "She's still listed in the book under 'Cecil Franks.' You'll find it in the book under that name. It's on Ferris Street."

There was a Cecil Franks listed at 1427 Ferris Street.

When McCall left city hall it was past noon. He found himself ravenous, which was usually a sign that he was troubled. His nose led him to a typical city hall-type restaurant around the corner by way of an aromatic blend of pig's knuckles, sauerkraut, noodle soup, and beer. On his way out he had to make a conscious effort to remember what he had eaten. It was after one when he parked at 1427 Ferris.

It was in the heart of Banbury's black section, the so-called west side. An indigenous Harlemite might not have recognized Banbury's west side as a ghetto, at least from its topography, although a member of the Watts community would have felt at home. It consisted mainly

122

of small one- and two-family houses neatly tended; its rodents were more likely to be field mice than rats. The occasional apartment building seemed neither as overcrowded nor as dilapidated as the multidwellings of the metropolitan slums. Under Mayor Potter, McCall understood, the city enforced health standards and tenement laws rigorously.

But if life in what Banbury's white racists contemptuously called Blacktown was more decently livable than in other cities' black enclaves, the area was nonetheless a ghetto. Under the surface rumbled all the bitterness, hatred, and unrest of the worst slums. A few had managed to burst the bars and through talent, industry, or luck insinuated themselves and their families into "good" white neighborhoods; the overwhelming mass were prisoners in Blacktown through realtor conspiracies, white community hostility, employment inequities, or their own conditioned submission and hopelessness. McCall felt a jarring buzz under the quiet air, as of the uncomprehended conversation of not an alien but an alienated people.

Fourteen twenty-seven Ferris was a small white green-shuttered house surrounded by a white picket fence. Two men came out of the house and pushed through the gate as McCall parked his car at the curb. He was surprised. They were Lieutenant Cox and Sergeant Fenner.

The lieutenant seemed just as surprised to see him.

"What are you doing here, Mr. McCall?"

"Looking for Mrs. Franks. You, too?"

"We've been searching her house for her brother Harlan's target pistol. I'm afraid she isn't going to throw her arms around your neck. We had to get a warrant before she'd let us look."

McCall said, "Find the pistol?"

Cox shook his head morosely. "James must have taken it along when he went into hiding. Although Isobel claims she never saw such a gun in his possession."

"She has to be lying," Sergeant Fenner snapped. "Harlan's lived with her about fifteen years, and that gun permit application was filed only two years ago."

"Kind of odd weapon to request a permit for," McCall remarked. "It's too long-barreled to carry about comfortably."

"Too small-calibered for decent defense, too," Lieutenant Cox said. "For snap shooting you want something that's going to stop the other guy even if you only hit him in the arm or a leg. And that means at least a thirty-eight. For precision shooting, of course, you can't beat a Woodsman. If you have time to aim, it's as accurate as a rifle. Up to fifty yards a good marksman could nail his target between the eyes."

"Yeah," Sergeant Fenner said. "It makes a lot better assassination weapon than a defensive one."

The two officers drove off, and McCall moved on up the walk. His ring brought the thin black woman to the door.

"What do *you* want?"

"Remember me, Mrs. Franks? I was in the detective bureau squadroom when the D.A. was questioning you about your brother."

"I remember you."

"Could I come in? I'd like to talk to you."

Isobel Franks said, "Look, Mr. McCall, I got nothing against you, you sounded like you were at least half on our side when that pig Volper was trying to push us around. But my husband, rest his soul, and my brother Harlan both always preached never to go along with a white man *no* way."

124

"Even if I want to help your brother?" McCall asked quietly.

"The rule is no white man no way," the woman said. "Sorry."

She slammed the door in his face.

SEVENTEEN

McCall stopped at a drugstore to consult a directory. LeRoy Rawlings's address was 1632 Compton. He looked at his street map; it was only two blocks east and a block south of the Franks house.

It turned out to be a four-family fake brick with individual outside entrances. The name Rawlings was on the letterbox of the downstairs right-hand flat.

A leathery old woman answered McCall's knock. She cocked her snow-covered head to one side like a wary bird.

"Yes, sir?"

"Mr. Rawlings home?" McCall asked politely.

"LeRoy? No, sir, he ain't."

"Any idea where I could find him, ma'am?"

The old woman seemed to relax. "I never know where that boy is. He never bother tell where he going."

"You're LeRoy's mother?"

"Yes, sir, Anita Rawlings."

"I'm Mike McCall, Mrs. Rawlings." He held his special shield case out for her to see.

She studied it for some time. "You a policeman?"

McCall realized that she could not read. "No, ma'am. I'm special assistant to Governor Holland."

Her eyes widened. "The governor of the whole state? Oh, my. Just you come on in, Mr. McCall."

McCall stepped into a sparsely furnished immaculate front room. From the old woman's nervousness, she had never entertained a white skin in her parlor before. She asked him if he would "set," and he chose an ancient leather chair with walnut arm rests that looked as if it had gone through the Civil War. She perched on the edge of her settee like a bird poised for escape.

McCall cleared his throat. He was casting about for something to put her at her ease, when a kettle began to sing somewhere. She jumped up.

"Excuse me, I was about to have myself a cup of coffee when you come," Mrs. Rawlings said. "I better turn that kettle off." She pronounced it "kittle."

"Don't let me stop you from having your coffee, ma'am," McCall said, smiling. "Fact, I think I could use a cup myself."

"You could?" the old woman asked, astonished.

"If you don't mind me inviting myself."

"Mind! Land sake. You just set there, Mr. McCall." She bustled out. "I'll be right back," she called.

McCall looked about. On the end table beside the settee stood a nine-by-twelve easel photograph in a gilt-decorated white Naugahyde frame; he rose for a closer look. It was a wedding portrait of a young couple, showing them from the shoulders up. The groom was stiff in a tuxedo. The bride was in a trailing veil. Both looked slightly frightened. The girl was dark, purely African; the man was LeRoy Rawlings.

"I see you been admiring my LeRoy's wedding picture," Mrs. Rawlings said. She was back with a pretty tole tray, obviously her best, bearing two cups of coffee and a creamer and sugarbowl. She set it down on her occasional table. "Here you are, Mr. McCall. Cream and sugar?"

"No, thanks, I like it black."

"*Everything?*" she said shrewdly, eyeing him.

"No, not everything," McCall said, grinning. "There are some I can do without—black *and* white."

"Now ain't that a fact," she said with animation. "You set, Mr. McCall!" She sipped her coffee.

"LeRoy's wife is a stunning girl."

"Not bad. I thought that boy would never marry. Going on two year now. My land, he all of twenty-eight 'fore he taken the step." She cackled and raised her cup again.

The lips and the shape of the jaw in the man's photograph could be those of Horton's killer, McCall decided. Could be. "Could be" was a long way from "were."

"Why the governor interested in my son, Mr. McCall?" Her sudden question startled him.

"It isn't LeRoy he's interested in, Mrs. Rawlings, I mean as an individual. Governor Holland sent me to Banbury to head off race trouble. And as vice president of the Black Hearts—acting president, now that Harlan James is hiding out—your son is in a good position to cool off the black brothers."

The old woman gave a bright nod. "If LeRoy and Harlan preach peace 'stead of preaching fight all the time, I like it finer. Don't get me wrong—I'm all for the rights we black folk win the last fifteen year. When I a young 'un, white people call me 'gal,' or 'Mandy,' treat me like I'm some kind of dirt. Now the white clerks in the stores say 'ma'am,' just like I'm good as the white ladies. LeRoy and Harlan say this never happen if not for the Black Hearts and such-like outfits, and I reckon they a lot to that. But all the time now they in trouble with the police. I like to die with fretting."

McCall said, "It's worrisome, all right, Mrs. Rawlings. Martin Luther King managed to win some important rights for blacks without violence, but I can see how lots of people would consider his methods too slow. Matter of fact, I've often thought that if I'd been born black I'd probably be a militant."

"You would?" she said. She appraised him with her direct black eyes. "Now ain't that interesting."

"I'm not saying I approve violence," McCall said quickly; no one was going to con this old woman. "I'm merely saying I think I can understand what drives black people to it. I know if I had to take the kind of pushing around the average black man does, I'd want to push back twice as hard, too. That wouldn't necessarily make it right. It's just that I'm mule-headed enough to understand your son's mule-headedness."

"Now, see?" Mrs. Rawlings said, smiling. "LeRoy and Harlan both wrong. They always say no white can understand how us blacks feel. More coffee, Mr. McCall?"

"Just about coffeed out," McCall said, "thank you. Heard from Harlan since he went underground?"

"LeRoy get one letter saying not to worry, but Harlan don't say where he at. 'Course, we hear him talk on the radio every day. LeRoy tune him on, or if he ain't here, Emily do. I wouldn't myself."

"You sound as if you don't care for Mr. James, Mrs. Rawlings," McCall said with a smile.

"Oh, I like him all right. But I hear that stuff so many times before. LeRoy and Emily always dragging me out to those Black Hearts meetings. Harlan a real fiery speaker, like an old-time preacher, but he keep saying the same thing over and over till you want to fall asleep. About the honkies, and the slavemasters, and all. I suppose it's true, but a body gets tired of the same old thing—"

The front door was keyed open suddenly and an attractive black woman in her late twenties came in. She was the girl in the photograph. She froze at sight of McCall.

The old woman said quietly, "Emily, this is Mr. McCall from the governor's office. My LeRoy's Emily, Mr. McCall."

129

McCall, on his feet, said hello.

Emily Rawlings's black eyes snapped. "You're the man who tried to get my husband to tell where Harlan James is hid out, aren't you?"

"That's right, Mrs. Rawlings."

She has styled her hair in an exaggerated Afro hairdo; the copper loops hanging from her ears were three inches in diameter. Her dress was violent and stunning.

"Get out."

The tiny white-haired woman said, "I declare I don't know where you brought up! Don't pay her no mind, Mr. McCall. The young folk today got no respect for nothing and nobody."

"It's all right, Mrs. Rawlings," McCall said. He turned back to Le Roy Rawlings's wife. "I just stopped in to talk to your husband—"

"The Black Hearts took a vote on you," the young woman said. "They decided the rule of no truck with pigs applies to you, too. So we don't want you smelling around our house. Like I said—get out."

The old woman was furious. "I going tell LeRoy about this! I sick of you and your uppity airs! Talking like that to a man from the governor hisself! LeRoy going to hear—"

"You do that," the young woman said, and flung the door open, holding it that way. "You heard me, Mr. McCall. Out. That polite enough for you, Mama?"

"It's all right, Mrs. Rawlings," McCall said again to her mother-in-law. "I understand this, too. It's been a pleasure and a privilege to talk to you."

She threw her apron over her face.

As he started his car, a motorcade began to creep across Jackson Road half a block away. He drove to the intersection and stopped to let it go by, assuming from its snail's pace that it was a funeral procession. But he was startled to see that most of the four to six men in each car were armed with rifles or shotguns. All were white.

The procession extended as far as he could see. There had to be well over a hundred automobiles in the convoy. Or posse.

Jackson Road was too narrow to allow him to drive alongside the procession. McCall backed into a driveway, returned along Compton, and took the first street paralleling Jackson. He raced for three blocks, then shot back to his objective.

The head of the procession was a quarter of a block away when he reached Jackson Road. McCall swung right, wheeled left, stopping his car broadside to the oncoming cars and blocking both lanes. He cut his engine and sprang out.

The lead car rocked to a halt; the cars behind it closed in bumper to bumper. The driver and three other men spilled from the lead car; they carried rifles. McCall recognized two of the men. The driver was the lanky blond man with the foreign accent whom Benjamin Cordes had called Zablonski. The man who had been seated beside Zablonski was the one with the red-veined doughface Cordes had called Rozak.

"What's the big idea, wise guy?" Rozak rumbled, brandishing his rifle. "You're blocking traffic. Get that heap the hell out of here."

McCall held his shield case up to Rozak's eye level. "What do you men think you're doing? Where are you going, Rozak?"

The man seemed taken aback. "How d'ye know my name?"

"I know this one's, too," McCall said. He glanced at the tall blond man. "Zablonski, who wants to wipe out Blacktown. Is that where you're headed?"

131

And where the hell were Chief Condon's police?

Zablonski blinked. "How this guy know me, Joe?"

"I remember now, Joe," one of the other men said. "I saw him at the union hall last night. He must have got your names then. Who is he, anyways?"

"Mike McCall," Joe Rozak growled. "The governor's errand boy. The hell with him." He whirled and waved the rifle over his head. "Nobody's going to stop us now, men! It's only the next block. Let's walk the rest of the way. Unload and walk!"

Men began to pile out of cars all along the line. In the confusion McCall innocently asked one man, "What's on the next block?"

"Black Hearts headquarters. Where you been? You want to get run over by about five hundred men, mister, you just keep standing here!"

Some of the men were making threatening gestures toward his car.

McCall glanced up and down the street. Except for the posse of whites, there was not a soul in sight. It was a street of small shops and neighborhood upstairs offices with plate glass fronts in a variety of lettering, much of it crudely done, with an occasional misspelling; here and there stood a three-story apartment building. There was no sign of life in the commercial establishments; it might have been Sunday. Apartment shades were drawn to the sills. McCall felt his flesh creep. The people here could not have had more than a few minutes' warning, yet it was as though the whole area had been evacuated by its inhabitants.

No vehicle moved, either, although the curbs were jammed with cars.

And the Banbury police were totally elsewhere.

A one-man army I ain't, McCall reminded himself.

He got back into his car, started the motor, backed around, and took off. None of the posse made an attempt to stop him. Joe Rozak was yelling orders, trying to get his army to form a column of fours, and his three lieutenants, headed by Zablonski, were hurrying back along the line to see that Rozak's orders were carried out.

EIGHTEEN

In the middle of the next block McCall spotted what he was looking for. Between a barbershop and a grocery store, an open flight of stairs led up to the second floor of a ramshackle two-story wooden building. Over the stairway hung a sign sporting a white circle with a black heart in its center, a white dagger thrust through the heart.

There was an alley beside the stairway, and McCall swung into it fast, jumped out of his car, and took the stairs three at a time. The door at the top was locked. He pounded on it. It opened three inches; it was on a chain. The face of LeRoy Rawlings stared out at him. There was a submachine gun in his hands.

"You crazy, man?" the vice president of the Black Hearts said. "You damn near got cut down just now. Get out of here."

"Let me in," McCall said. "Quick."

"What do you want?"

"There's a mob of maybe five hundred vigilantes headed this way, and they're armed to the eyeballs."

"We know it," Rawlings said. "We're waiting for them."

"Do you *want* a shootout, for God's sake?"

"That's up to the honkies, man. They want it, we'll oblige."

"Don't keep me standing out here," McCall urged. "Let me at least use your phone. Maybe I can still head this lunacy off."

"By calling the pigs?" Rawlings said. Somebody behind him laughed, and Rawlings grinned in response. "Well, why not? We'll get ourselves some pig meat, too."

McCall heard the rattle of the chain. He thrust with his shoulder and bulled his way past Rawlings. He was very careful to keep his empty hands in plain sight.

It was one large room, with peeling paint that had once been yellow and was now a streaky mustard brown. Graffiti decorated the walls. There were large posters of Malcolm X and Eldridge Cleaver. The floor was sagging, scuffed, uncovered. There was a six-inch dais at the far end, with a rickety table and three chairs. The front end of the room, where the windows were, bristled with guards. About twenty other men, all wearing uniform jackets with the Black Hearts insignia, were loading and checking carbines, shotguns, submachine guns. Boxes and clips of ammunition lay in heaps on the floor. There was no conversation.

Each face in the room was swiveled McCall's way.

He became very conscious of the color of his skin.

"Who invited the honky in?" demanded a light-skinned man; he had a handkerchief bound round his head and he was peering along the barrel of a .30-.30 which happened to be pointed at McCall.

"I did," Rawlings said. "This here is the governor's boy, *Mister* McCall. He wants to call the pigs to protect us from the honkies. A real big-hearted white man is what *Mister* McCall is. I say we let him. More targets."

"Do you have a bullhorn?" McCall asked.

"No, *sir*, Mr. McCall."

"Do you know where I can get one fast?"

"No, *sir*, Mr. McCall."

"No sound system, p.a., anything?"

"We po' black folks, suh. Ain't got nothin' but guns."

Everyone laughed.

"Where's your phone?"

135

"Why, suh, it's right over theah on that theah wall," the black leader said. "You got a dime, suh? 'Cause if'n you ain't, you's out o' luck."

Somebody spat an obscenity.

There was a pay phone on one of the walls. McCall had the dime out before he reached the wall. He jammed the dime in the dime slot and dialed Operator. Out of the corner of his eye he saw LeRoy Rawlings relatch the door and turn a key in the lock.

"Operator, this is a police emergency. Get me radio station BOKO, and get it fast."

He got the BOKO switchboard in twenty seconds.

"Ben Cordes. Emergency."

He looked around as he waited. He was in a cage of armed blacks, silently listening.

"Cordes speaking."

"Mike McCall. You said I could call on you if I needed help to head off a white-black explosion in this town. You know where the Black Hearts headquarters is, Mr. Cordes?"

"I've been there."

"How fast can you be here with amplifying equipment? I've got to address a mob. I want to sound like the voice of God."

"A white mob?"

"Your friends Rozak and Zablonski are leading it. My guess is they'll be here in ten minutes—they're forming a marching unit only a block from here."

"I couldn't possibly make it that fast," the station manager said. "Maybe fifteen. Have you called the police?"

"No. They should have broken up that posse, and they didn't. That tells me where your police force stands in this. Bring them in and there will be a slaughter. Our best chance is to talk the mob into going home. I'll try to hold them off till you can get here."

"On my way," Cordes said, and hung up.

McCall replaced the receiver and turned to the silent semicircle. The black faces remained expressionless.

LeRoy Rawlings said, in an altogether different tone, "We took you up in a meeting and voted not to cooperate with you, McCall."

"I know," McCall said. "I stopped by your house looking for you, and your wife told me. Look, men, I've got to head off this war. That's what Governor Holland sent me here to do. It's not only my job, it's a job I happen to believe in. Those whites out there are confused, afraid. They're as confused and scared as you are—as everybody is. They think one of your people murdered one of theirs. In their confusion and fear they're out for blood. I can't believe you people want to commit suicide. They're five hundred of them out there, each one with a gun."

"I would like to make the point," Rawlings said, "that it's them coming after us, not us after them. All we mean to do, McCall, is defend ourselves."

"Maybe it won't come to that," McCall said rapidly.

"You want to take the chance getting caught in a cross fire, that's up to you." Rawlings shrugged, but McCall thought he saw a very slight eagerness on the otherwise impassive black face.

"How come there are so few of you here? I was told you have several hundred active members."

LeRoy Rawlings smiled. He nodded toward the windows. Some guards moved aside, and McCall followed him over for a look.

The windows were covered by Venetian blinds, slanted to let the light in, but with the slats angled so that the men could not be seen from outside.

"Mainly they're two-story buildings in this block," Rawlings said. "Look close at the roof across the street."

McCall at first saw nothing. It was a flat-topped building with a low parapet around the perimeter of the roof. The usual small shops occupied the street level, and there were apartments on the upper floor.

Then a movement caught his eye. A dark face appeared briefly above the parapet. It turned in the direction of the white mob, then disappeared.

"You've got armed men on that roof?"

"A lot of roofs," Rawlings said. "The word went out just a couple minutes ago, but us Black Hearts are trained to react fast. When those honkies get here, they're going to have a hundred or more riflemen looking down their sights on them from roofs on both sides of the street."

McCall's stomach dropped. He had been trying to ward off a massacre of blacks. Now it appeared that the massacre was more likely to be of whites.

The tramp of marching feet came from the east. McCall saw a column of men, four abreast, advancing down the middle of the street. It was a ragged army. Some of the men had their weapons shouldered, others carried them at trail position; no one was keeping in step. At their head marched Joe Rozak and the man called Zablonski. Why they had ordered a column of fours seemed to McCall significant. It was a military formation, a symbol of discipline. Rozak or Zablonski—probably Rozak—therefore had qualms, if only unconscious ones, about what they were doing and sought the cover of legality for their illegal and dangerous operation.

"You know those two at the head of the column?" McCall asked Rawlings.

"Joe Rozak. Veech Zablonski."

"Veech? I never heard a name like that."

"A quarter of the honky guys in my high school were from Polish families. Veech is short for Vechek. Polish for Vincent."

"Veech Zablonski," McCall said thoughtfully, looking down at the blond rabble-rouser.

The man at his side grunted. "It may be carved on a tombstone in a couple days."

"Not if I can help it, Rawlings."

LeRoy Rawlings shrugged.

The column reached Black Hearts headquarters. Rozak and Zablonski fell out and stood aside, watching their army march by. As the vanguard neared the corner, Zablonski bawled, "Column—halt!"

The men came to a disorderly halt and, without waiting for another order, wheeled to face the building. Immediately they lost all semblance of order, dissolving their ranks and converging on the wooden building in their eagerness. Their two leaders screamed themselves hoarse, but the men paid no attention. In a few seconds all five hundred white men were crowded about the front of the Black Hearts headquarters.

A duck shoot, McCall thought, feeling sicker. All the black men had to do was lean over their parapets and empty their guns into the mass of whites below.

There was a rifle shot, and McCall jumped. Zablonski had fired his gun into the air to shock the men back to discipline.

In the mutter that followed, the blond man jumped on a trash can and waved his rifle.

"*Be quiet!*" he roared. "How we talk to the niggers when you act like bunch women at bargain sale?" He jumped down. "Okay, Joe. You take it."

Rozak climbed on the trash can. The red-veined face had paled to a sickly pink; his voice was unsteady. He shouted bravely, "LeRoy Rawlings! We want you! Come on down or we'll come up and haul you down!"

McCall said to Rawlings, "Any chance of your men opening up in a panic?"

The black leader shook his head without taking his

139

eyes from the scene below. "They have their orders. They're no undisciplined mob, like those stupid honkies down there. We shoot only in self-defense."

"Good," McCall said. "Now let me out."

"Out?"

"That's right. I'm going down to talk to them."

"Don't let him, Roy," a voice said behind them. "We got him, we can keep him for a hostage. Governor's boy. He's worth a lot."

"Not to those honkies down there," Rawlings said with contempt. "You want to die, Jesse?"

"I just as soon. What have I got to lose?"

"The only life you got. You're as dumb as they are. Let McCall out."

"You hear me, LeRoy?" Rozak was yelling. "You got just about sixty seconds!"

One of the men unlocked and unlatched the door. McCall stepped out on the landing. Zablonski spotted him from below and shouted something, pointing up.

Rawlings said from inside the room, "What you aiming to do, McCall?"

"Hold those jokers off till somebody they may listen to can get here. You're positive your men won't shoot unless they're shot at?"

"I told you, didn't I?"

"Better relock the door."

He started down the steps. He heard the door slam, and the sound of the lock and chain.

McCall halted at the foot of the stairs. The mob gaped; apparently the last thing they had expected was a white man. Rozak and Zablonski were glaring.

"Well, if it ain't McCall!" Rozak said. "You sure get around, McCall. What you doing in the Black Hearts headquarters? This here is Governor Holland's boy Friday, Veech."

140

"You leave Mr. Brown-Nose to me," Zablonski growled.

"Wait, wait," Rozak said. He shouldered his way a little past Zablonski, standing half between them. McCall noted almost with amusement, Rozak was a big bluff, a loudmouth adherent of popular causes who seized them in order to lead. It was Zablonski who was dangerous. "Why d'ye keep shoving your nose in, McCall?"

"I'm trying to keep a lot of people from getting killed," McCall said in an unexcited voice, but giving it a little extra projection to be sure to reach the whole listening crowd, "and you men from making damned fools of yourselves. This is a matter for the authorities, not a bunch of self-appointed vigilantes. I just talked to the police on the phone. In case anybody stops a bullet today, I wanted them to know whom to arrest for inciting to riot and murder. So I named you, Rozak, and you, Zablonski, as the ringleaders of this mob. You'll be the first they'll arrest."

Zablonski barked a laugh. "You hear that, boys? This bleeding heart, this snoop do-gooder, he didn't do his homework good. You think the cops give holler in hell what we do to a bunch of niggers, McCall? Have yourself a look. There."

He made a sweeping gesture toward the east with his gun.

McCall looked.

Two squad cars were halted at the intersection, facing toward them. The officers in the cars, unless they were wearing blinders, could hardly avoid seeing the weapons in the hands of the mob, or misunderstand the significance of the confrontation before the Black Hearts headquarters.

"They pick us up on other side of town, McCall," Zablonski said derisively. "Didn't stop us for spit. All they do over there is get ringside seat."

141

Stupid, it was all stupid. The officers must know that he, at least, would not hesitate to testify to their deliberate failure to act. Or—and McCall felt the chill again—was he slated to be silenced, too?

Zablonski shoved Rozak out of his way. "Okay, McCall. Get your butt out of here, or you just might stop slug with it."

McCall found himself working up to one of his rare rages. There was something about Zablonski that suggested an SS uniform and jackboots. He had to fight himself back to sanity.

"If you think you can get away with shooting an unarmed man in full view of hundreds of people, Zablonski, you're a bigger idiot than I think you are. I'm here with the authority of the governor of this state—it's the same as if Governor Holland were standing where I am. Go ahead and try your luck—I guarantee it will be all bad. Like the gas chamber, say?"

NINETEEN

The man showed his brown teeth. "We ain't going kill you, McCall, we just going walk over you if you don't get out of way." He turned his head and yelled, "Come on, boys! Don't let this crumb scare you!"

Gripping his weapon with both hands, he lunged for McCall and the stairway. McCall set himself. To retreat up the stairs would only heat the crowd's already steaming blood, the fuel of weakness that fires every pack hunting the kill. He had to stop Zablonski in his tracks.

"Veech Zablonski!"

It sounded like the voice of God, all right, rolling and echoing against the puny architecture. McCall thought, the U.S. Marines; and he let his breath out like an escape valve. A panel truck with a brace of amplifiers on its roof had charged up to the edge of the crowd. Lettered on its side was the legend RADIO STATION BOKO—*1410 On Your Dial.*

The driver of the panel truck was the redheaded station engineer and maintenance man, Andy Whalen, and Whalen was scared. But the other door was open and little Benjamin Cordes stood there, above the crowd, one foot on the seat, the other braced on the sill of the open window. McCall noticed that the hand gripping the microphone was white at the knuckles. He was as scared as Whalen, but the difference was that the little guy had guts. Maybe he'd make a good mayor at that.

"I'm not only talking to you, Zablonski, but to every man here. In case some of you don't know who I am, I'm Ben Cordes, and I'm running for mayor of Banbury. And I'm here to make a campaign speech."

143

The amplified voice boomed and pealed.

Someone in the crowd shouted, "Go home, Ben. We're for you, but this is no time to be making speeches."

There was laughter, and McCall thought, Now, Ben. Press your advantage.

"Isn't it? I've got news for you, friend. You're all set to blow it for me, you know that?" A puzzled silence settled over the mob. "I have the election cinched—or did have till just now—because the average voting joe backs my law-and-order stand. But if you think he wants mob rule, even by whites, you don't know the American voter. He simply won't go for a mob to govern him, white *or* black. You go ahead and shoot up these black citizens today, and I'll guarantee that public opinion will turn on a dime. You'll kill every chance I have to win the election. In fact, I'll guarantee your next mayor will be the black man who's my opponent. If that's what you want, Zablonski—and you, Rozak—and you, Collins—and you, Lennie Smith—" he kept picking men out of the crowd, stabbing at them with an accusing forefinger, so that each man so singled began to try to shrink out of sight "—okay, go ahead. But when your stupidity here today gets you a black police commissioner, and a majority of black cops, on top of a black mayor and a black city council, blacks running the city from top to bottom, why, then, don't come crying to me!"

Zablonski said sullenly, "It was your boss that nigger killed, Mr. Cordes. You want him get off free?"

"No, I want him caught and tried and punished," Cordes said. "But by the rules of law. You want the right man, don't you? If you blasted the head off every black in that building, would you ever be positive you'd caught and punished the killer of Gerry Horton? Break this up. Let the law deal with Horton's murderer. Or you'll boost Jerome Duncan into the mayor's office as sure as God made little green apples."

144

There was another pause.

Rozak said uncertainly, "Maybe he's right, Veech."

"Yeah!" someone cried.

"What about it, Zablonski?"

"I say we do what Mr. Cordes says—"

"Wait! Wait!" Zablonski roared. He was pushing his way toward the panel truck, followed by Rozak. When they reached it, Zablonski said something to Cordes and the little station manager turned off his microphone before replying. Zablonski argued heatedly; Rozak kept glancing at the roofs; Cordes listened, little head cocked, spoke in a soft voice. McCall was impressed.

He spotted a few black faces peering down at the crowd, but the Black Hearts posted on the roofs for the most part kept out of sight. McCall silently praised their discipline.

Finally Cordes turned the mike on.

"Veech Zablonski has decided I'm right. It takes a big man to admit a mistake. I want a hand for Veech!"

A roar went up from the warriors. Zablonski turned this way and that, nodding, smiling. Rozak looked sore about something.

"So will you all please get back to your cars in an orderly manner and go home the same way? And thank you men from the bottom of my heart."

God stopped booming to cheers, and the would-be slaughter was dead, stillborn. In twos and threes the men made for Jackson Road and their cars, talking animatedly.

McCall watched the two squad cars at the intersection. They did not move, forward or backward.

Observers. There to report the action.

Were they disappointed?

Their inaction could only have been the result of direct orders. It was inconceivable that neither team would have reported in by radio what was taking place, or

145

about to take place; at the least, they would have called for reinforcements. Banbury had a riot-control squad; where were they? The conclusion was disturbingly inescapable that someone higher up—could it have been Chief Condon himself?—believed in riot control only when the rioters were blacks.

Ben Cordes sat down in the panel truck and shut the door. Not once had he acknowledged McCall's presence on the scene. McCall grinned to himself. It would have been bad politics. Cordes was a canny old cookie. A tough man. It's so often the little guys, McCall thought.

Cordes had his driver, Whalen, remain where they were until the last white man was off the street and back on Jackson Road. Then the panel truck followed, like a cowboy after his herd. It disappeared, too.

The two squad cars suddenly came to life. One backed up and sped west. The other raced down the street past the Black Hearts building, siren blasting, turned north at the intersection, and rapidly faded out.

McCall waited peacefully.

Black faces began to appear above the parapets. McCall estimated that there were over fifty of them, all armed with rifles, carbines, shotguns. He could not see the roofs on his side of the street, but if there were an equal number above, Rawlings's estimate that more than a hundred riflemen would be at their elevated posts when the whites arrived had been no exaggeration.

The men began drifting out of McCall's line of sight, no doubt headed for the street. He heard footsteps behind him and turned around. It was Rawlings, hands in pockets.

They grinned at each other.

"Ben Cordes might have had a point there," the black man said. "Maybe I should have insured Duncan's election by letting that mob lynch me."

"There aren't many Nathan Hales in this day and age," McCall said, "of any color."

"Oh, I don't know. I could lay my life on the line for something I believed hard in—like, man, the Black Hearts. Not for a person, no."

"How do you stand on Duncan?"

Rawlings said evenly, "He's okay."

"Don't you want to see him win?"

"As against a honky? What do you think?"

"Any black man? Against any white?"

"Not an Uncle Tom. But any other kind of brother— sure . . . Why you looking at me that way?"

McCall had been staring at the lower part of Rawlings's face.

"I was wondering how you'd look with the upper half of your face masked."

Rawlings chuckled. "I've got five alibi witnesses."

"You would have those even if you were guilty."

"Sure. But it so happens that this time it's in the groove. We were having an executive meeting at the time Horton was hit."

McCall shrugged. He had been able to eliminate Jerome Duncan at once on the evidence of the black candidate's lips. But Rawlings's lips were quite thick—as thick, he thought, as the killer's. It was absurd to go on this way, anyway. Lips alone would not identify the man.

Black men were beginning to drift onto the street. Suddenly it was an everyday ghetto thoroughfare, peopled and humming. Children appeared, women.

May all wars end this way, McCall thought. Only the war hadn't ended. It was just a battle that hadn't come off.

"You've got to admire the way Cordes took over," he said. "All I wanted was his amplifying equipment. I didn't bargain for the voice of Jehovah."

"He's a honky," Rawlings said. "I think, McCall, you better light out of here while you still can. I wouldn't want anything to happen to the governor's boy."

"Do you know anything," McCall asked, "about a .22 caliber Woodsman? Owned, say, by Harlan James?"

Rawlings's strong chin stuck out suddenly; his big hands were balled. "That the kind of gun killed Horton?"

"Yes."

"I wouldn't tell you if he did. It just so happens, though, that he don't. Now you better take my advice before the brothers start throwing up at all that white skin you carry around."

He gave McCall his back. McCall decided to get out of there.

At a quarter of nine that night McCall slipped behind the wheel of the Ford. The exit of the hotel parking lot fed into Grand Avenue. He turned right off Grand, intending to take First Street north.

As he completed the turn he caught a glimpse in his mirror of something rising from the floor of his rear seat. A small round object pressed coldly into the back of his neck. A .22, McCall guessed. His right foot instinctively went to the brake.

The voice said, "Keep going to Taylor Street, then turn north." It was a man's voice, a whisper.

The headlights of an oncoming car gave McCall a glimpse of his captor in the mirror. The man was black, with bushy Afro-style hair. He wore a domino mask over the upper part of his face. Was it the man who had shot Gerald Horton? McCall was not sure from the one glimpse.

"What's this all about?" he asked in a calm voice.

"You oughtn't to get so nosy," the black man whispered.

He was disguising his voice. Why should he do that,

148

McCall wondered, unless he thinks I might identify it? Could it mean that he's not out for my blood—that he has a different purpose in abducting me?

"I'm nowhere near an answer to the Horton murder, if that's what you're worried about," McCall said in the same easy way.

"You got a rep for finding answers," the man whispered. "We ain't taking no chances."

McCall's spine reacted promptly. It sounded as though this was meant to be a terminal ride after all.

"Who's we?" McCall asked. "The Black Hearts?"

"Just keep driving."

They crossed First Street. McCall said, "Is this because of my visit to mama this afternoon?"

The man breathed, "Mama?" in a puzzled way.

"Mrs. Anita Rawlings."

There was a little giggle in McCall's ear. "You think I'm LeRoy Rawlings? That's funny. Taylor's the next block."

McCall carefully turned left at the corner. Taylor was a secondary street with little traffic and poor lighting. The gunman's choice of route was not encouraging.

"Okay, so you're not LeRoy," McCall said. "But is this snatch because of what I asked Mrs. Rawlings about Harlan James?" He added suddenly, "Or is it because I asked LeRoy about the target pistol?"

"It's because you got a nose like Jimmy Durante. What's this clue the cops have about the gun?"

"They don't confide in me," McCall complained. "Are you Harlan James?"

The giggle again. "If the cops didn't confide in you about the gun, we got nothing to talk about. So shut up and drive."

TWENTY

The man behind him directed McCall to continue to
Telegraph Road. McCall remembered it from his study
of the Greater Banbury map. Telegraph Road was at the
extreme northern edge of town. The edges of towns
tended to be sparsely populated places. The trip promised less and less.

En route they passed within two blocks of Laurel's
apartment house. McCall thought of it with nostalgia.

Once he saw a Banbury police car pull out of a side
street ahead of him and proceed at ten miles over the
speed limit. McCall increased the pressure on the gas
pedal. But the black man whispered, "Whatever you got
in mind, forget it. Stay behind, and don't make no
mistakes."

Half a mile later, the police car turned off. McCall
passed the corner with great regret.

At Telegraph Road the gunman directed him to turn
right. McCall was the soul of obedience.

A mile down Telegraph Road they passed the Banbury
city-limits sign. The terrain became quickly rural. Dense
woodland appeared. City lights had long since been left
behind.

The whole business seemed absurd. To go out this
way, at the hands of this crumb . . . McCall, you've had
a brief if glorious career . . .

A little over two miles beyond the city limits the black
man ordered McCall to turn into a narrow dirt road
hacked out of the woods. McCall's headlights hit a sign:
DOVER ROCK AND GRANITE CO.—NO TRESPASSING—VIOLA-
TORS WILL BE PROSECUTED.

"Don't pay no attention to the sign," the gunman whispered. "Keep going."

The road was truck-rutted, but it was dry and packed and looked old. Grass was high between the ruts. The trees crowded up on both sides, branches meeting overhead to form a ceiling from which the moonlight bounced off.

A quarter of a mile later they suddenly broke out of the leaf-roofed tunnel into a large clearing. It was a cloudy night, but there was enough moonlight to tell McCall that the place was an old quarry, with every sign that it had long ago been abandoned.

The dirt road ended ten yards from the pit. It was immediately apparent why the quarry had been abandoned. The diggers had hit an underground spring; the pit was full of water, creating a pool measuring about fifty yards square. The water came to within a foot or two of ground level.

"I used to swim here when I was a kid," the black man said in his fake breathy tone. "This pool's over a hundred feet deep."

McCall had never felt more alive.

"Cut your engine, the lights. Leave the key in the ignition."

McCall did precisely as directed. The puzzle was why the man was disguising his voice. It certainly didn't seem to indicate homicidal intentions. On the other hand, if he wasn't intending to kill, why this deserted quarry in a Godforsaken spot of forgotten woods? Maybe it was 'arf and 'arf. Murder on his mind, but the disguised voice just in case something went wrong. It didn't seem possible that the man was that subtle-minded, yet there it was, the only conclusion McCall could reach.

The whole train of thought left him tingling with a sense of accomplishment. Hurray for you, he said to himself gloomily. You'd be better off rehearsing your prayers.

"Come on. Pay attention."

He was conscious of a jabbing at his neck. Then the pressure of the muzzle eased and he heard the door behind him open. It automatically turned on the dome light. The gunman said, "Get out. But real careful."

He had backed off, well out of arm's range, as McCall opened the door at his side and slid from under the wheel. In the glow from the dome light he saw that the weapon in the black hand was a .22 Woodsman target pistol. The man was dressed as McCall had seen him the night before, in the meeting hall: black suit, black turtleneck Italian shirt. Even black shoes, which he had only guessed at in the hall. And the damn mask . . .

"Lean against the top of the car with both hands. Get your feet way back. Spread your legs."

The man's left hand did a clumsy body search. No police or paramilitary training, then. Or not likely. Funny how the brain kept ticking away like a computer, trying to figure it out. With death seconds away.

"I don't carry a weapon," McCall said. "I'm beginning to think that was a mistake."

"Shut up. Now drag out that stuff on the floor of the back seat. The chains first."

So it was to be murder. The whispering—a precaution.

McCall pulled his legs up, pushed away from the car, moved over to the open door at the rear. Lying on the floor, where the gunman had had his feet during the ride, was a set of rusty tire chains and a thin roll of piano wire.

"If this means you're intending to shoot me," McCall said, "you're out of your everloving skull. Do you know what Governor Holland will do if I'm murdered? On official business for him? The combined law enforcement

152

agencies of the state will go to work on the case. You wouldn't have a chance. Sam Holland will see to that."

"They'll have to find you first," the black man whispered.

"What are you whispering about? Dead men can't identify a voice."

"You ain't dead yet," the man said with an intensity that startled McCall. He was still whispering. "If you don't drag them chains out of there fast, I'll put a slug in your back on the spot."

McCall stooped to the chains. He half turned toward his captor as he dragged the chains out of the car, hoping for a chance either to swing the chains like a weapon or make a grab for the pistol. But the masked man had backed just far enough off to make either attempt suicidal. The muzzle was unwaveringly leveled at McCall's head.

The light from the car illuminated the face. From his stooped position McCall could see up a bit under the mask. The nostrils were wholly unlike those of LeRoy Rawlings, Jerome Duncan, or any other black man he had seen in Banbury.

He had seen newspaper photographs of Harlan James, the Black Hearts leader who had gone underground, and while news photos were usually unreliable reflections of reality McCall was certain these nostrils did not belong to James. In the photos he had seen, the Black Hearts president had a rather long nose.

McCall dropped the tire chains to the ground and straightened up. The pistol remained steady. It was trained now on his middle.

"Now toss me that roll of wire." The man held out his left palm. In the dim light from the car it glistened like black patent leather with sweat. *He's* nervous, McCall thought, and almost laughed.

He could not recall a time when his brain had worked harder, or faster, or to such little purpose. "Toss me the wire." If I could hurl it at his face and make a quick dive to one side at the same moment . . . The trouble was that the wire was too light to make an effective weapon. Even if it struck the gunman it would not stop him from squeezing the trigger. He could pull it at this range and be sure of putting a bullet into his captive's belly.

So McCall reached back into the car, got hold of the roll of piano wire, backed out, straightened up, and tossed the wire at the waiting hand as delicately as an operating room nurse handing a surgical instrument to the surgeon.

"Now shut the doors."

McCall slammed both open doors of the car.

"Won't do you no good making noise," the black man said. He was still whispering. "You could holler your head off out here and nobody'd hear you but the crows."

They stood in darkness now. Almost darkness. There was some moonlight, not much. Maybe I can use that . . .

"Tote the chains over to the pool."

McCall said, "If you're going to shoot me anyway, why should I do your work for you?"

"All right, if you want it now," the black man said. The muzzle came up again, steadied.

"Hold it!" McCall hurriedly stooped. He grabbed a tire chain with each hand and began to drag them toward the bank, going so fast that the black man shouted, "Stop or I shoot!"

McCall was within three feet of the bank. He dropped the chains and dived into the black water. Behind him the pistol cracked; he felt a sting in his right shoulder. Then the water closed over him.

It was cold. It was wonderful. My friend the water, he thought.

154

He struck out with powerful underwater strokes for the far bank. Naked or in swimming trunks he could have made the fifty yards without surfacing, but his clothes hampered him. He had to come up for air.

The pistol cracked again; there was a splash near McCall's head. The shot had come from the east side of the pool, not the south, where McCall had dived in. The gunman was circling the pool to be on the north side when he came out.

He dived again before the man could fire a third shot. Would he continue around the pool? Or would he anticipate that the swimmer would return to the starting point, and so be waiting there when McCall surfaced?

There was no time to engage in a long debate. The one thing he could be reasonably sure of was that the black man would not remain where he was. McCall struck out for the spot from which the man had last fired.

He knew there would be no time for a look around when he got to the bank. If he had guessed wrong and the gunman had remained where he was, it was curtains. There was no point in worrying about it.

The side of the pool was solid granite where McCall came up; it was cut as square as the edge of a swimming pool. His hands gripped the flat top of the bank and he heaved himself out of the water in one fluid maneuver. He bounced to his feet and was running a zigzag course for the nearby woods before the shot went off behind him.

From the direction of the report he realized that the gunman had done what he had anticipated: he had returned to McCall's starting point. Score one for your boy, Governor . . . He sprinted, squirting water at every step, almost enjoying the squishy sounds. Then he was under the protection of the trees.

McCall hugged a massive elm, gulping air. He peered around the bole in the direction of the pool. The cloudy

155

moonlight showed him that the gunman had moved to the southeast corner of the pool and was staring his way, no doubt trying to figure out in which direction his victim was fleeing. McCall stayed where he was, getting his breath back, waiting for the hunter's next move.

It might have occurred to the gunman that if he went blindly after McCall, the advantage of having the gun would be offset by McCall's being able to watch his approach, creating a possibly dangerous stalemate. It certainly occurred to McCall. He was just about to search for a piece of deadwood suitable for use as a club—the idea of lying in wait behind a tree until the gunman went past, then braining him from behind had its charm —when the black man solved everything.

He thrust the pistol under his waistband, dragged the tire chains back to McCall's car, picked up the piano wire, threw wire and chains into the rear, jumped behind the wheel, and drove off.

McCall waited for some time.

When he knew he was safe he left the sheltering tree and walked out into the clearing. He was suddenly aware of his right shoulder; it was stinging again, or at least he was conscious again of its sting. He probed gingerly. There was a rip in his coat and the pressure shot a jolt of pain into his neck and down his right arm. He decided that it was a mere graze. The cloth about the rip was not sticky; the wound had hardly bled.

He bent his attention to the problem of getting back to town.

The rutted lane back to Telegraph Road was risky; too much danger of walking into an ambush. The black man might have driven off with just that plan in mind—making McCall think he had given up, only to pull into the bushes somewhere along the dirt road, get out, and wait for the target.

McCall decided to stick to the woods.

It was mostly second-growth timber, with not much underbrush, so that walking would not have been difficult if he had been able to see. But visibility was near zero. The canopy of foliage shut out the moon's radiance as effectively in the woods as above the dirt road itself; McCall had to make his squishy progress in almost total darkness. He had always had an excellent sense of direction—he kept reassuring himself—and he set his course roughly parallel to the lane, or where his memory told him the lane lay. He was helped by the fortunate circumstance that it had been a straight road, hewn directly through the woods to the quarry.

He kept his arms before him, like a blind man, as a protection against low-hanging branches. Half a dozen times he fell over dead tree trunks and storm-pruned branches.

When at last he crouched behind a tall thick bush at the edge of Telegraph Road, he could not believe his good luck. He had struck it only about a hundred yards east of the entrance of the quarry road; he could see the big NO TRESPASSING sign glistening under the moon from where he was crouching.

If the black man had parked to ambush him, he was on the dirt road; McCall's Ford was nowhere in sight. Headlights were approaching from the direction of Banbury; there were no other vehicles on Telegraph Road.

He waited until the car passed, then darted across the road to the woods on the other side. He kept just inside the treeline, so that he had the road in sight, until the trees thinned out and finally gave way to open country, with no place to take cover except a ditch alongside the road. McCall dropped flat in it whenever headlights appeared from either direction.

When he reached the city limits he knew he was less than two miles from Laurel Tate's Ralston Road apartment. He headed for it, keeping to sidestreets and avoiding pedestrians as well as motorists. His appearance, if he were spotted, could only arouse curiosity or alarm, either of which could lead to a call for the police. He was not ready for that yet.

He cased Laurel's lobby from behind a box hedge; when he was sure it was empty, he slipped in. His waterproof watch told him it was ten past eleven.

Laurel was wearing a pink terry cloth robe that ended halfway between her knees and her hips; she was barefoot.

"Mike!" Her eyes widened.

"Do you always open the door at anybody's ring?" McCall asked.

"My God, Mike, what happened to you?"

"Latch that door." McCall stood in her tiny foyer dripping an occasional drop; his trek had evaporated most of the water.

"Is this the way you keep a date?"

"Sorry I'm late, but I've had a swim in an abandoned quarry, I've dodged a number of bullets, I've tripped over a number of dead branches, and I've just had myself a walk of about nine hundred miles in shoes full of water."

"I must say," Laurel said, "I've never heard a phonier excuse for standing a girl up, or it would be if I didn't have twenty-twenty vision. You get into that bathroom and take these filthy, sodden clothes off."

"Don't tell me you've got a man's complete wardrobe here for just such emergencies."

"I haven't even a robe that would fit you. But I'll fix you up with a blanket. Now git, before you have pneumonia all over my best rug!"

TWENTY-ONE

As he stepped out of the shower stall, McCall suddenly recalled the time he had had a like experience in the apartment of a girl in Tisquanto, the college town upstate. His substitute for a dressing gown on that occasion had been an oversized bath towel. It was now a pink blanket, but otherwise the circumstances were pleasantly similar. In Tisquanto he had arrived late for a date after a beating by a gang of stoned, naked juveniles. Tonight it was because of an attempt on his life. In both cases the girls had taken his clothes to launder and press while he was showering.

Remembering what had followed with the girl in Tisquanto, McCall found himself wondering if the aftermath of this shower would be equally enjoyable.

When he emerged from the bathroom bundled up in the pink blanket, Laurel had a board set up in her living room and was working away at his suit with an electric steam iron.

"I've pressed your tie," she said, pointing to where it hung over the back of a chair. "Your other things are in the washer. I set your shoes in the dryer, turned it on low and not tumbling, with newspapers stuffed in them."

"I can't complain about the valet service," McCall said. "Say, you're pretty handy with that iron."

"Your wallet and stuff are on the sink in the kitchenette. Maybe you'd like to spread the contents of the wallet out on the drainboard to dry."

"Practical girl." He headed for the kitchenette.

"Hey, big chief."

He halted in the archway. "If you're going to make bad jokes about my blanket, I'll take it off."

She wrinkled her nose at him. "I was just trying to attract your attention. You could mix a couple of drinks while you're out there. The liquor's in the cabinet under the sink and the mix is in the refrigerator. I'm bourbon and soda. What are you?"

"Strictly anything," McCall said, and continued his journey.

He was lying. For whatever reason—he had never attempted to probe the underlying cause—hard liquor held no allure for him. He liked neither the taste nor what it did to him, a sort of dehumanization, a pervasion of cold unemotionalism, that made him afraid of himself, of what he might do or not do under its influence. Consequently he drank as little as he could conveniently get away with. His work sometimes compelled him to keep up with a lush; in such cases he found no difficulty in doing so, always being astonished at his capacity. But he was relieved when it was over. He accepted moderate social drinking, as at present, as one of the minor irritations of life. It was always easier to share a couple of drinks with someone than to have to explain that he did not care for the stuff; people looked at him as if he were a freak or, worse, not altogether a man.

His change and pen were on the drainboard with his wallet. He tore several pieces of paper toweling off the roll above the sink and spread the contents of his wallet on them to dry. He wiped out the wallet itself and hung it over the dishtowel rack.

He made Laurel a stiffish bourbon and soda and for himself a gin and tonic, going easy on the gin. One of the advantages of gin was that, being colorless, it did not betray its relative weakness in his drinks when he mixed them himself.

She had finished pressing his trousers and was draping them over a hanger when he brought the drinks into the

160

living room. He set hers on a coffee table near where she was ironing.

"I don't think they'll shrink," Laurel said, taking a sip of her bourbon and then going to work vigorously on his jacket. "Now suppose you tell me what kind of wringer you fell into tonight."

He sprawled on her couch in the pink blanket and recounted his evening's adventure. When he reached the place in his narrative at which the gunman had fired at him as he dived into the quarry pool, she stopped ironing abruptly.

"You mean you're *wounded?* I thought that rip I mended—"

"Just a crease." He slipped the blanket off his right shoulder to show the two-inch welt; it looked like a burn. "I helped myself to your first-aid kit."

She went over to inspect it, then suddenly stooped to touch her lips to it. "Mama kiss the hurty place and make it well."

"I bit my lip, too," McCall said, and reached.

She dodged and retreated, laughing. "Later—maybe. Right now I'm busy ironing."

McCall finished his story.

She stared at him. "What's it all about, Mike? It doesn't seem to make any sense."

"I have a suspicion. I'll have to do some checking tomorrow before I express it. Because, if I'm wrong, I'd be wide open for a defamation-of-character suit."

Laurel tossed her auburn hair. "Meaning you think I'd go blabbing something you told me in confidence?"

"Meaning I don't want you thinking I'm an idiot," McCall retorted, "which you'd certainly think if my suspicion turned out to be wrong. It's that kind of suspicion."

"Now I am curious!"

161

"You wouldn't be human if you weren't."

"I wouldn't be a woman, you mean."

"And that would be a calamity. You know, with your pink robe and my pink blanket, we look like Hers and His?"

"Not *yet*, Mr. McCall," Laurel said firmly. "You just stay on that couch."

She finished ironing his jacket, hung it on the hanger over his trousers, and carried hanger and necktie into her bedroom. She returned wearing a pair of multicolored bunny-sized scuffs on her bare feet.

"Going somewhere?" McCall asked in an interested voice. He had ducked into the kitchen to empty his glass while she was in the bedroom.

"I have to run downstairs to the utility room. The wash cycle ought to be finished."

"I'll go down."

"Like that? You'd lose me my lease if any of my neighbors saw you. You can put up the ironing board, if you'd like. It goes alongside the fridge."

He was back on the couch when she returned with his shoes. She took them into her bedroom, announcing as she went by that his laundry was now in the dryer.

When she returned, barefoot again, she picked up her drink and unceremoniously sat down on his lap.

"You know, it's a few minutes to midnight and I have to get up at seven o'clock? So I don't think anybody will steal your clothes if we leave them in the dryer all night. Why, Mr. McCall, whatever are you doing?"

"Just replying to your kind invitation," McCall said.

Laurel slid her arms around his neck. "Would you care to elaborate?"

"Let's elaborate in the other room."

In the morning Laurel told him where to find a razor, and he shaved and dressed while she was fixing break-

162

fast. Afterward she drove him to his hotel before doubling back to city hall.

"Do you do return engagements?" she asked, at the marquee. "Or are you a one-night-stander?"

Beth McKenna had asked him the same essential question. Did he have telltale psychological odor, or was it a built-in radar linking all females?

He decided to be cryptic. That way lay discretion. "Am I invited back?"

She was equal to his ploy. "Are you kidding?"

"That doesn't answer me," McCall said, not without respect.

"Neither did your answer."

They both laughed.

"I'll be back," he said.

"I'll be waiting at the phone."

"You won't have to wait long."

There was remembrance of things recently past in her green eyes. "I didn't think I would."

When Laurel was gone, McCall decided to check the hotel's parking lot. He was not greatly surprised to find his Ford rental parked on the lot with the keys in it. There had been a good chance that the gunman had left his own car either on the lot or somewhere nearby before getting into the Ford to lie in wait, and if so he would have to come back for it. If McCall had not found the rented car on the hotel lot, he would have expected to find it abandoned in the vicinity.

The tire chains and coil of piano wire were not in the Ford. A few smudges of rust from the chains had rubbed off on the floor matting.

McCall drove to police headquarters. He ran into Lieutenant Cox and Sergeant Fenner in the lobby, on their way out.

"You fellows in a rush?"

"We have to go break the news to a burglary victim

that it was her own sonny boy lifted her jewel box," the lieutenant said in his sad nasal tone. "It can keep a while if you've got something more interesting for us."

"I got taken for a ride last night by Gerald Horton's killer, and I damn near got myself killed, too. Is that interesting enough?"

The two detectives stared at him. Sergeant Fenner muttered, "That's a cliffhanger for openers, all right. How about filling us in?"

When McCall had finished, the two detectives were silent. Finally Lieutenant Cox said, "Just because you've been nosy? The guy must be a kook. Or do you figure it some other way, Mr. McCall?"

"I'm not figuring anything till I've got more to figure on. Do you boys have any of the letters at headquarters here that Harlan James mailed to the Banbury radio and TV stations?"

"All of 'em. Plus all the taped speeches he sent with them. Confiscated them as evidence."

McCall turned to the sergeant. "Yesterday you mentioned a gun application by Harlan James that's on file. I assume he had to sign that?"

The sergeant nodded.

"You have a handwriting expert in your crime lab, of course?"

"Estes Clayton, one of the best," Lieutenant Cox said. "What are you getting at?"

"Let's have Clayton compare the signature on Harlan's gun application with the ones on his letters."

The two detectives looked at each other. Sergeant Fenner said, "That sounds like a more interesting thing to do, Lieutenant, than breaking the bad news to that society broad."

"You're very bright, you know that, Hank?" the lieutenant said. "All right, Mr. McCall, let's try it."

TWENTY-TWO

The gun registration files were housed in central district. Fenner fished out the application showing Harlan James's signature, and they all went up to the detective bureau squadroom to compare it with the letters.

McCall was disappointed when the application was placed beside one of the letters. The signatures appeared to be in the same handwriting.

"Don't let it throw you," the lieutenant said. "It takes an expert to tell even a poor forgery."

They took the comparison material up to the fourth floor crime laboratory. Estes Clayton turned out to be a professorial type, with square-shaped glasses and a bald head that made him look like Benjamin Franklin.

It took him two minutes with a magnifying glass to reach a conclusion.

"Crude forgeries."

"Crude?" McCall said. "I couldn't even tell they *were* forgeries."

"The signatures on all these letters are identical," the expert said. "No one ever writes his signature exactly alike twice. These have been traced from the same sample, probably an authentic signature." He added, "Not from the one on this gun application, though."

Cox and Fenner looked at McCall. "Okay," the lieutenant said. "Are we agreed on what this means?"

"I should think it was obvious," McCall said. "Where do we get hold of grappling equipment?"

"The fire department."

"The killer said the pool's a hundred feet deep. Can they go that deep?"

165

"Probably a fairy tale, Mr. McCall. My bet is it'll turn out to be less than fifty. You're convinced that's where James is hiding out?"

"My bet is I was supposed to keep him company."

Lieutenant Cox said sadly, "Can I use your phone, Estes? I have to call the fire chief."

Before leaving the fourth floor, McCall stuck his head into 401 to say hello to Beth McKenna. Unhappily, two nervous policemen were waiting to see Chief Condon, so there was no opportunity for conversation in depth.

Beth commented that she had rather expected to hear from him the night before.

"I was busy on the Horton murder," McCall said. Well, it was half true.

"Oh?" she said.

She waited.

McCall felt the thrill of caution that experience develops in bachelors of veteran standing. The cocked head, the whole attitude of that lovely body, reminded him of a hunter on the trail of prey, ready to get in the killing shot. The horrible part of it was that he was rather enjoying the sensation of being pursued.

"I'm not sure what my situation will be tonight, Beth. Things are coming to a head, and fast. If I should be free, are you available?"

"Oh, yes," Beth breathed. "I'm really amazed at myself. I seem to have no shame at all."

McCall glanced over at the two policemen, but they were too immersed in their own troubles with the chief, present and future, to pay any attention to office badinage.

He backed off hastily; that breathy delivery of Beth's held all the lethal promise of gasoline fumes in a match factory.

"I'll try to phone you before you leave for the day. That's five?"

"Yes."

"I should know how things are by then."

"I'll keep my fingers crossed," she crooned.

When he rejoined Cox and Fenner in the hall, he tried to recall just how his conversation with Laurel had gone when she had dropped him at the hotel. He remembered promising to phone her, but had he stipulated tonight? If he had, he was in deep trouble.

McCall led the way to the abandoned quarry in the rented car. Cox and Fenner rode with him. Behind them came the red car of the fire chief, and behind that the truck with the grappling equipment. At the scene it took some time for the dragging crew to set up. It was nearly noon before the operation settled down to business.

It turned out that Sergeant Fenner's estimate of the depth of the pool was good. The crew reported touching bottom at forty-five feet.

On the first drag, they hauled up debris ranging from a truck tire to a beer case; no bodies. The second try seemed fated to produce equally unsatisfactory results; McCall was beginning to doubt himself when the grappling hooks tangled with something heavy. The fire chief frantically signaled the man running the winch on the truck to put it in gear, and the object was slowly pulled to the surface.

It was the body of a man, and it was wrapped in tire chains. A black man.

The chains had been lashed in place by piano wire.

"There but for the grace," McCall said, looking down with distaste; they had deposited the body on shore. "This tire chain and wire deal seems to be the joker's standard operating procedure. Is this Harlan James, Lieutenant?"

"Nobody else," Lieutenant Cox said.

"He's awfully well preserved. I didn't think the water was that cold when I took my enforced swim."

"It must be a lot colder on the bottom," the sergeant remarked. "Where the pool's spring-fed."

They stared at the black man's corpse without pleasure.

"Somebody's been playing awfully funny games," Lieutenant Cox muttered. "The forged signatures on those letters I can savvy, but how'd they manage those taped speeches? They sounded like James's voice to me."

"They were," McCall said. "Only they were taped some time ago. James's orations were never very different. He had pretty much of a one-track mind—kept pounding on the same themes, using the same language. Somebody taped his spiels at the Black Hearts rallies and patched together fifteen-minute segments of them onto fresh tapes for delivery to the radio and TV stations."

"Rawlings," the lieutenant said. "It has to be LeRoy Rawlings—he was the one who delivered that first letter and tape to BOKO. That means if he didn't personally kill James, at least he had to know James was dead." McCall said nothing. "You don't buy it, Mr. McCall?"

"You certainly have sufficient grounds to pick Rawlings up for questioning. But I'd like to check out another angle before I settle for Rawlings."

"What angle?"

"One that could blow the whistle on this town. But I don't want to start tossing accusations around until I can prove them."

Sergeant Fenner scowled at his superior. "I told you, Lieutenant. This guy doesn't trust us."

"It's a matter of principle," McCall said, "not trust. You two will be the second to know when I'm sure."

"The second? Who's first?"

"Maggie Kirkpatrick of the *Post-Telegram*. I promised

168

her an exclusive. You have to hang around here, or can we head back to town?"

"Eager beaver, ain't he?" Sergeant Fenner said tartly.

"Shut up, Hank," Lieutenant Cox said. "We have to wait for the sheriff's crew, Mr. McCall. We're in the county's jurisdiction—this is outside the Banbury limits. Hank, go use Chief Menoski's two-way radio and get some sheriff's deputies over here."

Fenner made for the fire chief's car.

It was past one o'clock when the team from the sheriff's office arrived. The fire chief and the truck with the grappling equipment had left. It was lonely waiting in the old quarry with the body of the black leader. But, as McCall remarked, it was lonelier for James.

The county morgue bus pulled in while Lieutenant Cox and Sergeant Fenner briefed the sheriff's men. By the time the two city officers were free to leave, it was one-thirty P.M.; it was two before McCall and the detectives reached headquarters.

"Ever notice how hungry you get after you've gone through the bit with a stiff?" the lieutenant asked. "I'm starved."

"Me, too," the sergeant said. "It's the same at a wake. Everybody stuffs himself."

"Let's eat," McCall said briefly; and they swooped down on the police cafeteria. As they loaded their trays, McCall remarked that he had assumed they would put out a pickup order on LeRoy Rawlings the moment they got back. "Why didn't you, Lieutenant?"

"That mysterious angle you're going to check out discouraged me," Cox said. "We'll go talk to LeRoy, but you've got me half sold he's not our boy."

"Don't let me influence your investigation," McCall said.

"Haha," Sergeant Fenner barked. "You're a big help,

Mr. McCall, you are. If you ain't interested in that ham, sir, would you mind getting the hell out of my way?"

It was shortly after three when McCall parked before the radio station. He found the upstairs office of the station manager unoccupied. The monitor speakers were switched on, however, so Ben Cordes was probably somewhere in the building. A disk jockey was spreading his personality all over BOKO's air.

McCall went down the hall to the three studios. They were on the right side, so grouped that the window of the control room looked into all three.

A sound engineer wearing earphones sat before the control panel. Through the window McCall saw into Studio B, where the disk jockey was working. He was seated behind a turntable, chain-smoking; his feet were on the table where the record was spinning.

The door to Studio A was to the right of Studio B, the door to Studio C was to the left of the control room. The signs over both were unlighted.

McCall tried Studio A first; it was empty. He went up the hall to Studio C and quietly opened the door.

Cordes and Whalen, the redheaded maintenance engineer, were seated at opposite sides of a long table. Between them lay two tape recorders. The resonant voice of Harlan James was issuing from one, fulminating against Whitey for oppressing the black man. Since the reels of the other tape machine were also spinning, it was obviously re-recording the talk.

Both glanced up at once when McCall came in. Cordes immediately switched off the broadcasting machine; Andy Whalen switched off the other.

"Mr. McCall," the station manager–political candidate said. "We got another tape from Harlan James in the mail today. We're just re-recording it to cut out the profanity."

170

"You won't be getting any more tapes from Mr. James," McCall said. "He's dead."

"Dead?" Cordes seemed surprised. "Harlan James?"

"Harlan James."

Andy Whalen licked his thick lips. "Killed by the cops, huh?"

"No such luck," McCall said. "He was shot by the same skunk who shot Gerald Horton, weighted down, and sunk in forty-five feet of quarry water . . . *the same night he disappeared.*"

TWENTY-THREE

There was a lengthy silence. Then Cordes said, "That's not possible, Mr. McCall. James has been sending us these letters and tapes daily since he went into hiding."

McCall pulled out a chair at the end of the table and straddled it.

"The signatures on the letters were forged and the tapes patched up from old speeches he made at various Black Hearts rallies."

Whalen said excitedly, "LeRoy Rawlings! It has to be, because Rawlings delivered that first package!"

"I think Andy's right," the station manager said in a thoughtful voice. "Rawlings was also in a position to tape James's speeches, Mr. McCall."

"So were other people," McCall said, "any number of them. For instance, somebody doing research on the Black Hearts in a study of the black militant movement in this country. Or somebody else wanting a record of Harlan James's inflammatory statements for the possible future use of same by police, prosecutors, or politicians interested in putting the whammy on the Black Hearts. By the way, Mr. Cordes, how does it happen that you didn't recognize Rawlings when he delivered the package of tapes to your office here?"

Cordes blinked. "I told you. I'd never seen Rawlings on television."

"Maybe so. But you could hardly have avoided seeing him in person. Your late boss, Horton, told me you attended a number of Black Hearts meetings in the preparation of a special BOKO program on Banbury's black militant movement that you broadcast last month. It's inconceivable that Rawlings, the vice-president of the Black Hearts, wasn't present on at least one of those occasions. What's more, Rawlings as James's chief lieutenant would have to have been seated on the platform near his leader, just as you were seated on the platform near your boss Gerald Horton the night Horton was killed. In his executive capacity, in fact, LeRoy Rawlings probably even addressed these rallies, at least to the extent of introducing James. You had to have seen him, Cordes; you had to have known him by sight."

"Come on, McCall. What are you getting at?" There was a noticeable roughening of Cordes' voice, along with the dropping of "Mister." McCall felt relief. He shifted ever so slightly in the chair, balancing on the balls of his feet.

"Nobody delivered that first tape and letter to you, Cordes. You 'delivered' them to yourself. And mailed the tapes and letters received by the other stations, as well as the letter to Rawlings purportedly written by James. Where did you get the James signature you traced, by the way?"

The little man's eyes began to go this way and that.

"I imagine he had something with his signature on it in his wallet when you grabbed him. He must have had a driver's license, a credit card . . ."

He stopped. Cordes had suddenly got to his feet and walked over to the glass partition separating the studio from the control room. He pulled down the black shade, barring the view of the sound engineer. McCall was busy watching Whalen; the ex-boxer was a physical threat.

Cordes did not reseat himself; he stood glaring down at McCall, who nodded toward the twin tape recorders on the table.

"You were putting together another speech to 'arrive in the mail' tomorrow when I walked in. You don't have to re-record a speech onto another tape to blip out an undesirable word here and there. You can simply erase on the original tape. I took you by surprise and you had no time to think up a better explanation for what I caught you doing. It was careless of you not to lock the studio door."

The station manager glared at his maintenance engineer; his maintenance engineer glared back. "I was here first," Whalen said sullenly. "I naturally thought you—"

"*Shut up,*" Cordes said. His little hands were fists now, and he planted them on the tabletop, transferring his glare from Whalen to McCall. "Do I understand, McCall, that you're trying to implicate me in whatever happened to Harlan James?"

"I'm not trying," McCall smiled. "I've done it."

"You're out of your mind! Next thing I know you'll be accusing me of having murdered him!"

"No, Cordes, only of masterminding his murder. And, of course, of being behind Gerald Horton's murder, too."

"You are plain, raging mad!"

"Actually, I've been kind of slow on the uptake. If it weren't for that Milquetoast front of yours, I'd have given you at least a passing thought when I was thinking over possible motives for Horton's murder. But you were so beautifully reluctant to take his place as mayoralty candidate. I have to admire—if that's the word—your timing, Cordes. Coming only a week before the deadline for filing candidacies, Horton's assassination left no time for the party to groom anybody but the departed bigwig's shy and faithful right arm, his campaign manager, strategist, and speechwriter. You'd actually helped draft the party platform. Who else was there who could step in at the last moment and hope to make a creditable race of it against the black candidate? You knew that no matter how hard you shied away from a draft, the party's executive committee would force you to accept the candidacy; you were their only possible choice."

174

"Words," Cordes said; his nose was pinched white at the nostrils. "Hot air. Meaningless!"

"Horton's killing was timed beautifully for another reason, Cordes. The way you inherited his top spot on the slate more than made up for the handicap of not being very well known to the voters. You knew that the majority of the white electorate, scared by the assassination, wouldn't stand for black militants getting their candidate in—or, anyway, a black man—by killing off his opponent. They were bound to vote against Jerome Duncan if only to show the black community that such tactics wouldn't get them into power. Your plot to have the white candidate assassinated by a black was diabolical, Cordes. It could have produced one of the bloodiest race riots of this century."

"You must be stoned," Cordes said. "High on grass or something. It would have been a lot better for you, McCall, if you'd make these ridiculous accusations with no witness present. Andy, I want you to remember every word this lunatic's said, because I'm going to sue him—and that unscrupulous upstate politician he works for!—for defamation of character. By God, McCall, I'll sue for a million dollars!"

"Why don't you both sue?"

"What?" Cordes said.

"What, what?" Whalen said. "What d'ye mean?"

"You're going to have grounds, too."

"What's that supposed to mean!"

"You should have taken a course in makeup from a qualified actor, Andy. Or done some research on the nearest member of the Black Hearts. When you held out your hand at the quarry to catch that roll of piano wire, your sweaty palm glittered like patent leather. Don't you know there's far less pigmentation in the skin of the black man's palm—and the soles of his feet—than in the rest of him?"

The silence became ghastly.

Whalen said weakly, "I don't know what you're talking about . . ."

"You're accusing my maintenance engineer of having made up as a Negro and killed Gerry Horton?" Benjamin Cordes yapped. "Who'd believe a wild yarn like that?"

But McCall went on evenly, "At your instigation, Cordes. And then you sent him after me, although you must have had some doubts about Andy's ability to do the job, because you had him make up in blackface again just in case he wasn't able to pull it off and I survived to give the police a description of my abductor and assailant."

"You're guessing!"

"No. On the way to the quarry my 'black' kidnaper asked me what the clue was that the police got from the pistol used by Horton's killer. I'd mentioned the existence of a clue to only three people: Mayor Potter, Jerome Duncan, and you. To the mayor and Duncan I said nothing about the gun, only the bare statement that the police had a clue. It's true that the mayor could have learned about the pistol application report on James from Chief Condon—assuming Condon had had a report on it from Lieutenant Cox and Sergeant Fenner—but even if he had, the mayor is a wise old fox who doesn't go around running off at the mouth to potential killers. And yes, Duncan could theoretically have been involved with the killer—but how could he have known that the clue I mentioned concerned the weapon, which has never even been found? That narrowed it down to you, Cordes, and to you I *had* made a slip and specified that the clue concerned the weapon. So I figured: who's close to Ben Cordes, a white man with thick lips and broad nostrils? Why, his handyman Andy Whalen."

Whalen said thickly, "I'm going to sue him, too!"

"You'll have to try it from a jail cell, I'm afraid,"

176

McCall said. "Once Cox and Fenner run all this down, they won't have any trouble putting the tag on you, Whalen. There can't be a lot of places in or around Banbury where you can buy or rent the kind of Afro wig you wore, and the fact that you're white will have stuck in the storekeeper's memory. And how many places are there in this town where you can buy theatrical makeup? On top of that, you've probably got the stuff stashed away in your home, including that black Italian shirt and the Woodsman pistol, in case your boss here wants you to go into character again. Incidentally, *was* that Harlan James's target pistol?"

Whalen's face was as red as his hair. "I don't have to listen to this—" He jumped up.

McCall stood in his way. "If you think you're going to rush home and destroy the evidence, Andy, forget it. The only place you're going is police headquarters."

"You going to stop me?" Whalen roared. "You think you're as good as Kid Cooley?"

"That's history, Andy, ancient history. Look at your pot. Anyway, I'm not getting into a boxing match with you; your fists probably still rate as lethal weapons in the law books. I'm merely reminding you that running away isn't going to solve your problems. The law will collar you no matter how fast and how far you run. So use your head and come peacefully."

Whalen lunged and threw a whooshing left hook to McCall's jaw. But McCall was faithful to his gym regimen; he saw the paunchy ex-fighter's punch coming in slow motion, and he was inside it harmlessly and jabbing with the stiffened fingers of his right hand into the man's exposed armpit. Whalen yelped; his left arm came down like a tree trunk, temporarily paralyzed by the judo jab. He bellowed a curse and tried a right cross to McCall's head. The smaller man ducked inside again, grabbing the offered wrist with both hands like a drowning man

177

He whirled, yanked, and flipped Whalen over his shoulder. The ex-pug landed on his back with a mighty crash.

And he lay there, heaving for air.

"I said I wasn't going to box you," McCall said. "But I didn't promise not to defend myself. Are you all right?"

"Put up your hands, McCall," said the voice of Benjamin Cordes behind him. "Slow and easy."

McCall thought it the better part of valor to obey implicitly; Cordes sounded cold, bitter, and convincing. He turned with his arms raised. The station manager-candidate must have had a gun in his desk drawer. It was a very businesslike-looking .38 revolver, and it was directed at McCall's belly.

"Do you really think this is going to get you anywhere, Cordes? The police know everything I've told you."

"I doubt it," the little man said. "I think you came here to kind of feel me and Andy out first. We're finished if you did tell them, anyway, so we may as well operate on the hope that you didn't. Lean against the edge of that table with both hands. No, McCall, you know better than that. Feet spread and well back."

Cordes stepped over behind McCall, ran his left hand down and around McCall's body. He did a professional job; McCall wondered where he had learned.

"I don't carry a hand gun," McCall said. "I could have saved you the trouble and me the undignified stance, if you'd only asked."

"You can straighten up and turn around now." There was no relaxation in Cordes's tone.

When McCall turned around, Cordes was standing six feet away, beyond arm's length. McCall's respect for Cordes's know-how increased. And for the .38 trained on his middle. He even knows that, McCall thought. A man could survive a chest or a head shot; many did. But a gut shot at close range with a big caliber gave you pause, for

178

the most part permanently. In between times it was very painful.

Andy Whalen sat up on the floor. He seemed dazed. Or was it disbelief? He got laboriously to his feet, massaging his left arm.

"It'll be all right in a minute or two," McCall said.

"Your cool sickens me," Ben Cordes said. "Shut up! Andy, is your right arm okay?"

Whalen mumbled something. He was glaring at McCall with mayhem in his eyes.

"Then take this revolver." The little man gave it to Whalen. "Guns make me nervous."

McCall doubted it. The shy Milquetoast was of course an act. Too bad, he thought, I didn't spot that when I could have done something about it.

Cordes cracked the door open, glanced up and down the hall. He pulled it wide. "I don't think anyone else is in the building but Banner and his sound man. You keep McCall covered every second, Andy; he's tricky. I'll lead the way."

They took the back stairs down. The stairway ended at a door with an upper pane of glass. Cordes took a long, careful look at the parking lot.

"Wait here with him," the candidate for mayor instructed his muscle man. "I'll back the panel truck right up to the door in case somebody comes out onto the lot from the back of the furniture or clothing stores. Leave this door shut, Andy, till I get the back door of the truck open. Then load him in fast."

TWENTY-FOUR

Through the glass pane McCall saw Cordes climb into the driver's seat of the panel truck. The lettering on its side, RADIO STATION BOKO—*1410 On Your Dial,* did not reassure him.

Cordes backed the truck to the building. He got out and strolled over and opened one of the truck's rear doors. He took a casual glance about. Then he yanked the building door open and said urgently, "Move!"

McCall had hoped for a break here. The ramming muzzle of the .38 between his fifth and sixth vertebrae dissuaded him; any break at this point would be enjoyed by his captors, not by him. He moved.

Cordes slammed the door behind them.

The inside of the truck remained well lighted. Not only was the rear windowed, but there was a broad area above the cab of the truck that was open, admitting light from the front, too. The left side of the interior was completely taken up by a panel of electronic equipment, dials, meters, and a jack for earphones. The truck, McCall saw, must be utilized as a mobile broadcasting unit, covering news events at the scene.

The right side was occupied by a bench. McCall seated himself on the end nearest the cab. The earphones that plugged into the panel on the other side were lying on the bench at this point; McCall's body hid them from Whalen's view. He let his right hand rest on them, and as the big man half turned to latch the rear doors McCall quickly hefted the phones. He sat them down noiselessly and immediately.

They were just heavy enough to enrage the redhaired

killer into firing if they caught him square in the face; the odds against incapacitating him with the headset were too great.

Whalen sat down at the other end of the bench, near the doors. He was slued around on his right buttock, the .38 pointing at McCall. His glare said, "Try me."

The exit from the parking lot was into the side street. Cordes turned right to Grand Avenue, then right again. He drove a couple of blocks before turning right a third time. So he was heading north.

Over his shoulder Cordes said to Whalen, "You'll have to give me directions to the quarry after we hit Telegraph Road."

"We can't use that. If they found the nigger's body there, it's lousy with cops."

The truck slowed. "Yes." Cordes sounded thoughtful. Not worried at all. "Do you know another good place, Andy?"

"Head out that way, anyway. There's another dirt road into the woods hardly anyone uses."

The truck picked up speed.

"Take Taylor Street north," Whalen said. "There's less traffic."

Cordes shook his head coldly. "First Street will be faster." Interesting. He apparently felt that he had lost face by having made the mistake of heading for the quarry. At a time like this, when he was scheming for his life, he was still concerned about asserting his leadership. It took a dangerous man to do that.

They rode along in silence. In a few minutes they turned into First Street. Into heavy traffic. McCall saw Cordes's little jaw tighten. He glanced at Whalen, who was looking triumphant. But the big man said nothing.

"You should have carried a gun like this last night, Andy," McCall said. "Not that silly little popgun."

Whalen glanced down at the revolver in his fist. He

181

grinned at McCall. "That Black Hearts nigger—Harlan James—was toting the target pistol the night of the snatch when I cold-cocked him. We figured maybe it'd come out that James owned a pistol like that, so we decided to use it on Horton."

"Why don't you learn to keep your mouth shut?" Cordes said.

"What difference does it make now?" Whalen growled. "He ain't going to be talking to anybody except St. Peter."

Cordes opened his mouth. Then he closed it. After a moment he laughed. It was the kind of laugh McCall could have done without. "That's a fact," the little man said.

"I admit it wasn't very smart using it to put the snatch on you, though," Whalen said; he was feeling better now, beginning to enjoy himself. "With this in my mitt last night, like you say, you'd be laying in a hundred feet of water right now."

"I'd be lying in forty-five."

This irritated Whalen. "You said that before! Where'd you get forty-five from?"

"From the people who measured the pool," McCall said, "when they fished James's body out."

"Damn!" This official news seemed to bother Whalen. He muttered, "They always said it was over a hundred."

"Forget the pool!" Cordes shouted suddenly. "You've got to direct me, you know. Watch the road! And watch McCall."

"I'm watching him," Whalen said sulkily. "*And* the road."

"You'd better! It's our hides that are at stake here, and never forget it."

There was another silence.

McCall said suddenly, "How did Cordes con you into

this dumb play, Andy? Okay, so he wanted to be mayor of Banbury instead of manager of a lousy little radio station and the guy behind the political scenes. But what were you going to get out of it? I mean that rates big enough to risk a murder rap?"

"I get a soft city job, and when he moves up to the governor's pad I get me a top state job, where there's plenty of payoff."

"You . . . blabbermouth!" Cordes yelled.

"Ah, it's like talking to a stiff," Whalen said. "Keep your cool, Ben. What's a little chin-chin with a dead man?"

"And which job," McCall asked, "did he promise you when he becomes President? Secretary of Defense?"

"If you don't button up, McCall, so help me I'll have Whalen spatter your brains all over the truck!"

McCall sensibly buttoned up. He had been chattering more as a diversion than for information; Whalen's promised payoff had been predictable enough. For some time now he had been noticing, past Whalen's shoulder, through the window insets in the rear door, a gray sedan about two years old, a Pontiac that looked quite ordinary. But what it was doing was not ordinary. It manipulated the traffic in a peculiarly persistent way, remaining several cars behind the panel truck, managing to keep its position in spite of cross streets.

He had become quite interested in the gray Pontiac. Just about as interested, he thought, as Sir Galahad in the Holy Grail.

When they turned into Telegraph Road, the Pontiac followed suit. McCall wondered if desperation and the need to wish for a miracle were not making him see pursuit by the gray sedan when the likelier reason for its behavior was that both vehicles were simply traveling in the same direction at the same speed.

183

Whalen glanced back at intervals, but he seemed to be looking for landmarks. He did not appear to notice the gray sedan.

At the city-line marker he said, "The quarry road's about two miles ahead. Watch for a sign on the left, Ben, saying Dover Rock and Granite Company."

"I thought we weren't going there," Cordes said. He sounded strained.

"Just use it for a landmark. About a quarter mile afterward there's a dirt road to the right. Kids use it as a smooching place. You'll have to watch close, because it's easy to miss."

McCall groped for the earphones again. A three-foot cord terminating in a plug was attached. McCall felt for the plug and despaired. It offered less utility as a weapon than the earphones.

Cordes muttered, "There's the Dover Company sign."

"Then start watching for that lover's lane. Slow down, slow down."

The truck decelerated. McCall felt a twitch of hope when the gray car slowed, too. Why was the Pontiac decelerating in unison with the panel truck if it was not a tail? On a lonely road, with little traffic?

"I see it!" Cordes slowed even more.

McCall's heart plummeted. The gray sedan picked up speed, overtook them, and shot by.

Goodbye tail.

Goodbye world was more like it.

The panel truck swerved and turned into a dirt road. It was a bumpy dirt road. Even on their rumps he and Whalen lurched about on the bench . . . not much time now.

McCall suddenly found himself supremely calm. He had never felt clearer-headed in his life. Maybe it's because there's so little of it left . . . forget all that. Concentrate on the immediate present.

With the lurching of the truck as a cover, he wrapped the plug end of the cord around his right hand.

What have I got to lose? Maybe two-three minutes of living. It had been ridiculous to worry. Death couldn't come this way. Not to Mike McCall. Death was something that came to other people. A world without Mike McCall was unthinkable. Easier to imagine like McCall without a world.

Through the rear window he studied the terrain. The road was similar to the one that ran to the old quarry. Rutted. Narrow. Bordered by overarching trees . . .

"This ought to be far enough in," Cordes said. His throat sounded dry. It almost amused McCall. He thought: He's more nervous than I am.

Andy Whalen slued his battered face around to squint out the rear window.

Now.

McCall whipped the three-foot cable in an arc like a cowboy. The earphones at the cable's end whirred. He leaned forward and let fly. The cord struck the wrist of Whalen's right hand, the one grasping the .38, eighteen inches behind the earphones. It lashed around the wrist three times faster than a rodeo champion tying a bull calf's legs. Immediately McCall threw himself back, jerking with both hands.

Whalen was yanked forward to his knees. The revolver boomed once. The noise in the confined space was like a blow.

McCall sprang and laid a lefthanded judo chop across the back of the man's thick neck. Whalen collapsed to the floor on his face and lay still.

Unwinding the cord from his hand swiftly, McCall scooped up the .38 and swung around in a crouch.

But Benjamin Cordes still faced forward, he still gripped the wheel with both hands.

Then, deliberately, he toppled over on the seat. There

185

was a growing red stain, like an accelerated motion picture of a rosebud, neatly in the middle of his back.

The wild shot from the .38 had pierced the back of the driver's seat and buried itself in his spine.

McCall was standing beside the panel truck when the gray Pontiac raced up the lane. Sergeant Fenner jumped out from behind the wheel, and Lieutenant Cox hit the dirt from the other side. Both had Detective Specials in their hands, and both looked first at the .38 in McCall's hand.

"So that was you tailing us," McCall said. "After all."

"I see you did all right on your own," the sergeant grunted. He was leaning into the cab. Cox was looking into the rear of the truck through the doors McCall had opened. Whalen was still out; McCall had lashed his hands behind his back with the cable.

"We've been on you ever since you left headquarters," the lieutenant said. "We'd have lost you if the truck hadn't swung past us on Grand Avenue, though. We were waiting out front, watching your Ford. Ben Cordes driving a BOKO wagon with his own two little hands made us curious, so we decided to follow. Cordes got hit?"

"Cordes," said Sergeant Fenner, straightening up, "is cold mackerel. They're going to have to get themselves a third candidate for their ticket."

It was almost five P.M. by the time McCall had phoned Maggie Kirkpatrick her promised exclusive, Andy Whalen had been booked in central district, and he himself had completed and signed his statement in the detective bureau squadroom.

McCall was not surprised by a message from Chief Condon to stop into the chief's office as soon as he was finished.

McCall found Mayor Potter with Condon in the outer office. Beth McKenna was typing at her desk, trying not to look overjoyed.

The chief's face looked like the map of a mountainous country. "Terrible thing, terrible," he was rumbling. "Ah, McCall. I tell you, Mr. Mayor, it's going to blast this town apart like an atom bomb. McCall, I asked you in to explain personally to the mayor. I don't want him to have to wait for the official transcript of your statement."

McCall sat down in the chair beside Beth's desk. "Excuse me for sitting down, Mr. Mayor. I'm a little pooped—"

The old man waved impatiently. "You're not hurt, are you?"

"Just my ego." And McCall gave a laconic account of the day's events. Beth had stopped typing and was listening shamelessly.

"Cordes and that redheaded maintenance engineer of his?" The aged mayor shook his head. "Is there enough evidence to convict Whalen and implicate Cordes as the instigator?"

"I understand that Lieutenant Cox and Sergeant Fenner just found Whalen's black-man outfit in his house, and Whalen's sung like an opera star. It's a wrapup, Mr. Mayor."

"I still say it's a terrible thing," Chief Condon growled.

"Why, Chief?" the mayor asked. "It's going to cool off the hothead whites—maybe it will even make some of them feel shame when they learn that it was white men who planned and executed the murder of Gerry Horton and tried to frame a black man for their crime—and it's certainly going to boost the morale of the black community when a white man gets his just deserts for once. Or are you worried, Chief, that this is going to make Jerome Duncan Banbury's next mayor?"

"You don't think that's going to tear this town apart?"

the chief cried. "You won't catch me serving under a black mayor!"

"No problem, Chief," the mayor said dryly. "You can always resign and move to South Africa."

"Don't think I won't!" Condon shouted. "The way this country's going to hell—" The rest was lost in the slam of his private office door.

"I should have fired him long ago," the mayor said comfortably. "Oh, Laurel."

"I finally caught you," Laurel panted. She had run in carrying a stack of typed letters and envelopes.

"Sorry to make you chase me all over town," the old man said. "But these letters have to go into the mail tonight."

"Would you like to use my desk, Mr. Mayor?" Beth asked, rising.

"Thank you." He sat down with the letters and calmly began to sign them. Laurel stoood by folding and enclosing them in the envelopes as he signed. She had given McCall one brief smile, which vanished when her eyes turned to Beth.

"Well, Mike," the mayor said, signing away, "I don't suppose, now that the excitement's over, you'll be with us much longer?"

"There's no official reason to linger," McCall said carefully, "once I phone in my report to Governor Holland."

"I haven't even had a chance to give you a feed. As a grateful public official I'd like to end my incumbency on a historic note—toasting the man who saved Banbury. Could you possibly make dinner tonight?"

McCall glanced swiftly at Beth, hoping that Laurel would not notice. Beth gave him the briefest understanding nod, releasing him from their date. He could have kissed the old man.

"Yes, sir," he said. "I'd be honored."

At which Mayor Potter promptly said, "I've already

invited a very old lady-friend of mine to dine with me this evening, Mike. So you'd better bring a girl of your own. Do you know any in town?"

McCall shut his eyes against the looks of expectancy in two pairs of lovely feminine eyes, the green and the blue-violet.

How do I get out of this one? he thought. Lucky Sam Holland! What I need is a troubleshooter to solve *my* problems.

Then the solution occurred to him. "I really owe a certain newspaperwoman in town a date," McCall said.

"Maggie Kirkpatrick," the mayor nodded. "Nice girl, Mike. And smart. By all means."

And who knows? McCall thought, smiling at the four furious eyes turned his way. Maybe afterward . . .

189

If your dealer does not have any of the MAGNUM EASY EYE CLASSICS, send price of book plus 10 cents to cover postage to MAGNUM CLASSICS, 18 East 41st Street, Room 1501, New York, N.Y. 10017.